MONTANA MAVERICKS

Welcome to Big Sky Country, home of the Montana Mavericks! Where free-spirited men and women discover love on the range.

THE TENACITY SOCIAL CLUB

In rough-and-tumble Tenacity, it seems everyone already knows everyone else—*and* their business. Finding someone new to date can be a struggle. But what if your perfect match is already written in the stars? Pull up a barstool and open your heart, because you never know who you might meet at the Social Club!

Josh Aventura is as solid as they come, a rancher you can count on to have your back or mend your fence. But his friends jokingly call him the President of Lonely Valley, until he meets beautiful Amy Hawkins, a rodeo rider used to city lights and world travel. Josh's tenderness heals Amy's aching heart, but he fears they're on borrowed time—and he wants Amy for keeps.

Dear Reader,

In the small town of Tenacity, Montana, you'll find good hardworking people and Split Valley Ranch—the perfect place for sunset horseback rides across the pastures. It also happens to be a place where romance comes alive for Amy Hawkins and Josh Aventura.

Burned by love, Amy is only looking for a place to escape the limelight of her failed relationship, but what she finds instead is something even better. Josh has closed himself away, focusing on his ranch, until he meets Amy—who changes his life completely. But are they each willing to risk their heart again after going through so much pain in the past?

Amy and Josh remind us that opening up yourself after heartbreak is one of the hardest yet most rewarding things you can do, and that's something I think we can all relate to a little bit.

I am so excited to share Amy and Josh's story in my first Harlequin Montana Mavericks novel. I hope readers fall in love with the new characters who call Tenacity home, and enjoy reconnecting with old ones. So here's to second chances, dear reader, and to believing that the next best thing is just around the corner. If you enjoy this new addition to the Montana Mavericks series and want to talk handsome cowboys, you can find me on Instagram @elizabethhrib, swooning over my favorite books, or at elizabethhrib.com.

Elizabeth Hrib

ALL IN WITH THE MAVERICK

ELIZABETH HRIB

MONTANA MAVERICKS

Special thanks and acknowledgment are given to
Elizabeth Hrib for her contribution to the
Montana Mavericks: The Tenacity Social Club miniseries.

MONTANA MAVERICKS

Recycling programs
for this product may
not exist in your area.

ISBN-13: 978-1-335-14320-4

All In with the Maverick

Copyright © 2025 by Harlequin Enterprises ULC

Harlequin Enterprises ULC
22 Adelaide St. West, 41st Floor
Toronto, Ontario M5H 4E3, Canada
www.Harlequin.com

Printed in U.S.A.

Elizabeth Hrib was born and raised in London, Ontario, where she spends her nine-to-five as a nurse. She fell in love with the romance genre while bingeing '90s rom-coms. When she's not nursing or writing, she can be found at the piano, swooning over her favorite books on Instagram or buying too many houseplants.

Books by Elizabeth Hrib

Montana Mavericks: The Tenacity Social Club

All In with the Maverick

Harlequin Special Edition

Hatchet Lake

Lightning Strikes Twice
Flirting with Disaster

Visit the Author Profile page
at Harlequin.com for more titles.

Chapter One

Amy Hawkins knew a thing or two about working dangerous jobs.

As a rodeo star, she'd been bucked off the back of horses, slammed into gates by the roughstock, and stared down by bucking bulls. But stocking shelves at Strom and Son Feed and Farm Supply—the store owned by her sister's fiancé, Caleb, and his father, Nathan—was proving to be even more dangerous than getting between a cow and its newborn calf.

In the six weeks she'd been at the Tenacity, Montana store, she'd learned not to separate a grumpy ranch hand from his feed order. What she hadn't apparently learned yet was how not to mix up said orders.

"What happened now?" Faith said as Amy ducked behind the cash counter, using her sister as a human shield to hide from the surly man marching through the store with Caleb.

His face was beet red, his eyebrows pinched in a tight knot in the middle of his forehead. Amy couldn't tell if the color was from working out in the sun or if he was huffing and puffing over getting a truckful of feed back to his ranch before realizing it wasn't what he ordered.

"I might have sent the wrong order home with the MacPhersons."

"Not again." Faith checked the computer above the cash

drawer, the corner of her mouth twitching. "That's twice in two months."

"In my defense," Amy said, staring over her shoulder, "the MacPhersons' and the McPetersons' orders always show up at the same time."

Faith smirked, flicking her long, dark braid out of the way as she made an adjustment to the online order. "I'll handle it. Can you finish ticketing the clearance items in aisle two for me?" She passed Amy a roll of yellow stickers, each of them indicating a twenty-five percent markdown.

"Sure you wanna let me handle that alone?"

"Really? You can rope a calf in seven seconds but you can't put some stickers on some feed bags?"

"Of course I can. I just think it's funny when you get all those stress wrinkles across your forehead."

Faith smoothed her hand across her forehead, glowering at Amy. "You're lucky I like you," she said as Amy waltzed away. "Because you are definitely our worst employee!"

"I don't know… Pretty sure Caleb's angling to make me employee of the month."

"Doubtful."

Amy turned around and framed up a square with her fingers against the wall. "I think my face would look great right behind the register."

"As if. We might put your face up there as the first person ever fired from Strom and Son."

"Firstly, you're not paying me. This is free labor. So remember that when you try to fire me. Secondly, you'd miss me too much."

"Miss you hogging our guest room," Faith muttered as Amy walked away grinning.

To be fair, Faith had done Amy a huge favor, inviting her down to Tenacity. She hadn't quite known what to expect of the little hardscrabble town in Montana, but when Faith offered her the guest room, Amy had eagerly accepted. After a bad breakup, she'd been desperate to escape Bronco, leaving the crowded city and social media scene behind in exchange for some small-town refuge. From what Amy had seen so far, there wasn't much going on in Tenacity, and that suited her just fine. Spending time with Faith and putting some work in at the store was about all the social activity she could handle right now. Besides, she'd learned recently that there were worse things than stocking shelves and ringing up orders for surly cowboys.

Heartbreak was certainly worse.

And rejection.

And finding out that the person you thought you loved had up and gotten married while you were apart.

That was definitely worse.

So, as far as Amy was concerned, stocking shelves was a dream come true.

There was something almost calming about stocking shelves. Maybe it was the repetitiveness of the motion. She appreciated the neatness and the order. She liked that everything had a place. Surprisingly, she also enjoyed the quiet, even if it meant taking the occasional order from Faith. If someone would have told her all that six weeks ago, she'd have laughed them right out of a rodeo arena. Now she was starting to crave the slower pace in Tenacity. The monotony. And especially the distance from her whirlwind life.

Amy stopped in front of a stack of feed bags, double-checking the brand before she started tabbing them with yellow stickers.

"Amy?" Faith called from somewhere in the store.

Strom and Son Feed and Farm Supply was a large, boxy building with shelves upon shelves of anything a rancher could ever need. There were bags of livestock feed for a variety of animals—cattle, sheep, goats, pigs. But also grain and fresh hay and corn. The building always smelled faintly sweet, a little like home if Amy was honest, which probably had something to do with how much time she'd spent mucking out horse stalls growing up. There were also feed buckets and salt licks and horse tack and an aisle with toys for enrichment.

"Yeah?" she said.

Faith appeared at the end of the aisle.

"Nathan said the new April shipment of feed came in. He's gonna get the guys to unload the pallets. Help me with inventory when they're done?"

"Sure thing," Amy said. Despite the earlier feed order mix-up, she'd been a quick study with Faith as her guide, and she was starting to know the business like the back of her hand. They made a good team, which wasn't surprising, considering they'd spent a lot of their life traveling the world's rodeo circuit together along with their other sisters, Tori, Carly and Elizabeth, before settling in Bronco not long ago. Because of that, they often fell into a natural rhythm, one that reminded Amy of being on horseback and barrel races and rope tricks.

To look at them, it would be hard to tell they were sisters. Faith had high cheekbones, beautiful dark brown eyes, clear brown skin, and was only about five foot two. Though what she lacked in height, she made up for with her spunky attitude. Meanwhile, Amy was almost five foot seven, white, with bright blue eyes and straight, shoulder-length brown hair she left loose unless she was riding. Frankly, Amy didn't share looks with any of her sisters. She didn't even share DNA, considering they were all adopted. But the way they could read each other and the way they all loved fiercely—

those were the things that made them family. The Hawkins Sisters had always been known as a group of strong rodeo-riding women, and Amy liked to think they lived up to that.

Or, at least, she had. Amy had only been away from the rodeo for a short time, but some days she felt like a completely different person. Was that what Faith saw when she looked at her now? Someone looking to step out of the limelight? While living in Bronco had been nice, it wasn't exactly a quiet existence. With more of her family settling in the city, The Hawkins Sisters had become the talk of the town. It had become almost impossible for Amy to go out in public without being recognized.

But Tenacity was different. Here she didn't have to traipse around in sunglasses and baseball caps all the time, and most days she could forget that Truett McCoy—the cowboy turned actor whose posters graced the walls of young fans around the world—dumped her to run off and marry his costar back in February.

There were moments when that realization still hit her hard, though she did her best not to mope. Faith would only worry more than she already was.

Amy finished up her task and headed back to the cash desk to return the roll of unused stickers. As she did, she turned up the radio, the song ringing out over the store speakers. She hummed along, grabbing a small bag of feed to return to a shelf in aisle four. When the song finished, the radio hosts started chatting, and it took Amy a moment to understand why the hairs on her arms had stood up.

"Can we talk about everyone's favorite cowboy for a second?" one of the hosts said.

Amy knew immediately that they were talking about Tru.

"Oh my gosh, yes!" the female host said. "Let's."

"Okay, last we heard, Tru McCoy was linked to several

women prior to his whirlwind marriage. Isn't that right, Cady?"

Amy glowered at the shelf. There was only one thing worse than falling for a cowboy, and that was falling for a cowboy turned movie star. Of that, she was certain. In recent years, Tru's name above a marquee virtually guaranteed a box office smash, and his popularity had skyrocketed. Everyone was talking about him. After the breakup, she'd avoided the magazines and the trashy entertainment news channels, but apparently she'd forgotten about the radio.

"Wasn't he also supposedly seeing some unknown rodeo star?" the male host said. "We all know Montana is bustling with them."

Amy bristled. That's all she was in the end? Just an unknown, unnamed rodeo star? Her chest constricted, and she felt like a fool. Damn Tru McCoy, and damn him again for making her feel this way. She blinked back the tears she could already feel gathering in the corners of her eyes. She couldn't keep letting him affect her this way.

The host continued. "But apparently none of that matters because according to sources, his heart has always belonged to his new bride. Isn't that sweet, Cady?"

"Almost as sweet as you, Doug. And we definitely like a man who knows what he wants. We'll be right back after the break."

What he wants? Amy thought. Ha! Anger pooled inside her. It was no wonder her emotions had been all over the place since arriving in Tenacity back in February. Just bringing up Tru's name made her a weepy, blubbering mess, never mind being reminded that she'd been second fiddle all along. It was embarrassing and insulting. But what was even more mortifying was her reaction to the news after this many weeks. She'd been through breakups before. And she likely would again. She just needed to stop thinking about Tru. All it did was upset her and exhaust her, and she couldn't spend all her time trying to sleep away these feelings.

"And we're back," the radio host announced. "Talking about everyone's favorite heartthrob, Tru McCoy."

Hearing that she was only one of his many women shouldn't have surprised her—this was what happened when you fell for cowboy-hat-wearing movie stars. But the tears still threatened to spill, and Amy tugged a little too hard on the bag of feed she was putting away. It slipped from the shelf suddenly, sliding right through her outstretched hands.

It hit the floor, splitting at the corner, and the feed poured out all over her shoes in a dusty pile, sending pellets and grain dancing across the aisle. Amy swore under her breath. At least, she thought it was under her breath. It must have been louder than she thought, because Faith appeared a moment later and that made her tear up harder.

"Everything okay?"

"It's all good," Amy said. "Just a little accident. No big deal, I've got it." She did her best to avoid Faith's eye. Though they'd never discussed her fling with Tru, and Faith had never directly asked about him, Amy suspected that she knew. Sisters always knew these kinds of things. It was one of those special powers they were gifted with. That and the ability to annoy you in three seconds flat. Still, mortified at her reaction, Amy shook off the tears and hurried to the supply cupboard to grab a broom.

What did they say? Never cry over spilled milk? And here she was almost crying over spilled cattle feed. If anything, Amy should be ecstatic that she'd dodged that Tru-shaped bullet. He'd clearly never liked her despite his many declarations, and the last thing she needed to be was tied to a snake of a man. She was more grateful than ever that they'd used protection when they'd finally slept together back around Christmas. She'd even taken a pregnancy test to be sure because she'd felt sick right after the breakup, and with her birth control, she hardly ever got her period. With that worry assuaged, now Amy was mostly just angry for getting caught up in Tru's charms in the first place. She wasn't naïve. She'd lived and breathed the celebrity world for most of her life. She should have known better than to trust a cowboy with a handsome smile.

Amy swept the spilled feed into a pile, then dragged over the garbage bin, crouching to scoop grain onto the dustpan.

A set of footsteps drew near. Amy looked up, expecting Faith, but instead she saw a man—talk about a cowboy with a handsome smile. His hair was cut just above the shoulders. Dark brown, like his eyes. It was the kind of hair that looked especially good swept back under a cowboy hat. Much like the one he carried in his hand. Not that she was thinking of cowboys. Nope. Amy had strictly sworn off cowboys. But with his dusty blue jeans and snug T-shirt and olive complexion, she couldn't help but stare. He tilted his head, his gaze lingering, and for a moment, Amy wondered if he'd recognized her as one of The Hawkins Sisters. He wandered a little closer, and she prepared for the question, wincing internally.

"You know," he said. "If you get a couple of chickens in here, they'd take care of that for you no problem."

Amy blinked up at him, then she laughed, caught off guard by his comment. It was a real, deep belly laugh. She couldn't even say why she found it so funny, but as the sound faded between them, she almost couldn't remember why she'd been such an emotional mess. "You're probably right." She got to her feet. "Unfortunately, we're fresh out of chickens."

"You sure? You checked the back?"

"Almost positive. The only chicken you're going to find back there is Faith's chicken salad sandwich."

"Probably not as helpful in that form."

Amy bit her lip. A *funny* cowboy. Now that was a dangerous combination. "No. I wouldn't say so." She glanced at the flatbed cart he'd left at the end of the aisle. "Do you... Can I help you find something?"

"I'm looking for a fortified cattle feed. It used to be over there by the door."

"Oh, right," Amy said, leading him out of the aisle and toward the far end of the store. "We're doing some rearranging of the stock. Well, Faith and Caleb are. I'm just a lowly grunt worker."

"As if," Faith snorted from behind the cash desk as they passed. "I'm not forcing you to be here. Hi, Josh," she called, waving to the man that followed Amy.

Josh, huh?

"I do good work for you," Amy replied. "You should appreciate me more."

Faith smiled a little smile. "I guess I shouldn't bring up the earlier order mishap or the fact that you just wasted an entire bag of feed?"

"Take it out of my nonexistent salary," Amy teased.

Faith crossed her arms, smirking. "I just might."

Amy reached the far aisle and turned down it, lifting her hands in a kind of ta-da motion. "Here you go. Not sure which kind of feed you're looking for, but all the fortified ones are here."

"Thanks," Josh said, scanning the shelf. "I haven't seen you around before," he added before she could walk away. He grabbed a couple bags and tossed them on his cart. Thick veins ran up his muscled forearms. "Uh..."

"Amy," she supplied. "I came down to visit Faith back in

February. Haven't really gotten around to leaving yet, so I figured I better earn my keep."

He smiled at her. It was a soft smile. The kind that might get her heart fluttering under different circumstances. He had one dimple in his cheek and lines by his eyes that told her he smiled often.

"And you?" she said. "You must not come by the store a lot."

"Only about once a month," Josh said. "To stock up on supplies. Sometimes I have Caleb arrange to deliver the larger orders if I can't get away."

That was likely why they hadn't crossed paths yet. "Get away?" Amy prompted.

"From my cattle."

"You have a ranch?"

"Yeah, Split Valley." He raised his hand and gestured in a vague direction. "Up on Juniper Road?"

Amy bit her lip and shrugged. "I'm not super familiar with town yet. I haven't been out much if you don't count the store."

"Right," Josh said. "Well, Split Valley Ranch used to belong to my parents. When they retired, I took over."

"Carrying on the tradition?" Amy said. She could appreciate that. She and her sisters had rodeoing in their blood.

"The Aventuras have been on that property for as long as anyone can remember."

"Josh Aventura," Amy said, mostly to herself. "Do you have any horses up at this ranch or just cattle?"

"A few horses. Makes getting around the property easier at times if I don't need to take a truck out for repairs or something. And it's easier to round up wayward cattle. Plus I just like to ride. Have ever since I was a boy." He pulled another bag of feed off the shelf and added it to his cart. "What about you? Ride much?"

Amy almost laughed in his face. Did rodeo star Amy Hawkins ride? Her brows rose. He really had no idea who she was. *What a treat*, she thought, her gaze traveling up his forearm as he reached for another bag of feed. Her eyes landed on his biceps before she managed to tear her gaze away.

"You never answered my question," he pointed out.

"I do ride," she said. "It's actually one of my favorite things."

He flashed her a smile. "Yeah?"

"Yeah." This was usually about the time she'd say something about the rodeo, and his eyes would get wide as realization struck. *A Hawkins Sister! Of course!* But Amy bit back the rest of her explanation. It was refreshing having someone be interested in her without the name attached. Without knowing who she really was.

"So you came down to visit from… Where? Bronco?"

"How'd you know?" she asked.

He flicked his head in her direction. "Just a guess. But you look like a city girl."

Amy glanced down at her attire. Sure, maybe her jeans were a little more expensive than what they wore around here, and her button-down was high-end, but she blended. Right? "What about you? Ever been to Bronco?"

He nodded. "A few times, especially when I was younger. But with the ranch I don't have a lot of time for traveling."

That was understandable. Amy suspected he also didn't have time for a lot of things, like TV and radio and following what Tru McCoy was getting up to. He seemed like the type of guy who could really care less about Hollywood gossip. Where Tru had to be the center of attention in every room, Josh struck her as a little gruff, a little quiet. And with his dusty boots, there was certainly nothing flashy about him. He really didn't seem to have any interest in charming anyone, certainly not her, and maybe that's exactly why Amy *was* so charmed by him.

Faith had been telling her for weeks to get out of the house and meet people. Amy had brushed her off more times than she could count, but right at this very moment a part of her strongly considered asking Josh out for coffee. It had been a long six weeks since everything had ended with Tru, and Josh seemed like he might be interested in her enough to say yes. If she could manage to pry him away from his cattle.

But as she watched him load the last few bags of feed onto his cart, she reconsidered. She no longer felt like she could trust her own judgment after the Tru situation. Maybe Josh was just being friendly. Tenacity was small; people took a genuine interest because they cared, not because they were trying to flirt. Maybe she'd read far too much into a handsome smile.

"Ready?" she said as Josh finished up. "I can ring you up at the cash desk."

Josh nodded. "I think that's everything."

They walked to the front of the store together. Amy stood behind the register and totaled Josh's order.

Josh paid, his eyes lifting to meet hers briefly. Amy tore the receipt free and handed it to him. She might be mistaken, but for a second he seemed to linger, like he wanted to ask her something. Then he just smiled and said, "Good to meet you, Amy. I appreciate all your help today."

"Of course. I was happy to. If you don't mind telling Faith that the next time you see her," she teased. "I'm gunning for employee of the month."

"Well, I don't know how you could possibly have competition."

"That's what I keep saying."

They chuckled and Josh ducked his head, that dimple in his cheek deepening as he pushed his cart across the store. Amy watched him until he disappeared out the door.

"You know," Faith said, coming up behind her. She leaned her chin on Amy's shoulder. "I think that's the most words I've ever heard him say in all the time he's been coming in here."

Amy glanced at her. Faith wore that shrewd look she got when she was sussing something out.

"I'm serious. The best Caleb and I usually get is a polite grunt of acknowledgment. If Iris is around, sometimes she'll inquire after his parents and he'll give her a nod and a shrug." Iris was Caleb's mother. "Personally, I didn't even know the man was capable of that much conversation."

"Oh, come on," Amy said.

"I think he liked you. Who knows why?"

Amy scoffed. "Rude."

"You should have asked him for coffee."

"I was just being nice. *He* was just being nice."

"You asked if he had horses. You were getting down to the things that matter."

Amy laughed. She did have a soft spot for a man who loved to ride as much as she did. "I was trying to get you a sale. Now Caleb's gonna have no choice but to put my picture on the wall."

"We're probably not gonna see Josh back here for a month. You have four weeks to work up the courage to ask him out."

"Why are you so obsessed with me getting out to meet people?"

"Because it's good for you. And because you can't sit home every night watching *90 Day Fiancé*."

Amy made a vague hum of agreement. She was developing quite the evening routine. "I really was just trying to be friendly."

"You could have continued being friendly over coffee."

"Your suggestion is noted and I have chosen to ignore it."

"I swear I'm setting you up with the next single cowboy that walks in here."

"Good luck with that," Amy said.

"You know, sometimes I have good advice," Faith said, walking around the counter as a customer flagged her down for help. "You should listen to me every now and then."

"What was that?" Amy said, reaching to turn up the radio again. "I couldn't hear a word you said."

Faith rolled her eyes. "You're thirty-five. I thought you'd outgrow being annoying by now."

"And that assumption was your first mistake." Amy planned on annoying Faith well into old age. But even as she stood there, knowing it was best to leave handsome cowboys alone, she couldn't stop her thoughts from straying back to Josh.

Chapter Two

There was something special about a Montana spring.

Josh knew that the mountains would still be covered in snow, but every day the valleys grew more lush and green, filled with the buds of new wildflowers. The snowfall had been heavy this year, forcing Josh to start the herd on hay to supplement the leftover forage the cattle nosed at from the previous growing season. But even the acres of land around his property had started to flourish, allowing him to finally move the cattle on from winter feeding activities.

Now the ranch was in the thick of calving season which usually began at the end of February and wrapped up in early May. As a boy Josh had learned not to get attached to the new little additions to the herd, and though he still heard his father's words echo in his head—*these aren't pets, son, they're our livelihood*—Josh maintained that all these calves running around the property as the world blossomed made his heart light.

Or maybe he was particularly thoughtful today.

Perhaps that was it.

Spring made him think of new life and new life made him think of family, and he imagined what it would be like to have what his father had: a woman he could adore and a kid (or a couple) that he could dote on. When Josh's dad had finally retired and handed the ranch over to him, it came with a piece of advice. He'd said that at the end of the day, all that really mattered was not what Josh did with the land, but that he had good people to call home. *Not a place*, he'd said. *People*. At twenty-four, when Josh had been given the ranch, he hadn't thought much of that. He'd been determined to carry on his father's legacy, to make Split Valley Ranch something he could be proud of, and he'd jumped into the sweaty, backbreaking work with all the vigor of a young man. But now he was thirty-six, and Josh was thinking about his father's words a lot lately.

Mostly he was thinking about the way his last relationship had crashed and burned. Josh didn't think he was asking for too much, but so far life hadn't been kind to him as far as romance was concerned. In fact, he'd had his heart kicked around a cow pasture a couple of times. Frankly, he'd prefer to be the night-calver for a whole season, stuck waiting up all night for heifers that might have trouble birthing, more than he would like a repeat of that dating experience. Josh had sort of come to terms with the fact that this was his lot in life: his land and his cattle.

So why couldn't he get Amy out of his head?

"What's your deal?" his friend Noah said from the other side of Josh's truck as they loaded the bed with supplies. Josh had noticed some downed portions of the fence when he was driving into town the other day and Noah was here to help with the repair. The cattle weren't currently using that pasture, but it was best to repair these things when he found them. If not, he'd forget about it in the chaos of the ranch until he drove out to find the cattle on the road one day.

"What are you talking about?"

Noah shrugged. "You're quieter than usual. That's all."

"And that's saying something!" Noah's brother Ryder

laughed. He crossed the porch, a toolbox in his hand, clunking down the steps in his work boots. "What he actually means is you're brooding worse than a hen."

Noah inclined his head toward Josh as if to say *he's not wrong.*

Josh sighed, leaning against the bed of the truck. Noah and Ryder Trent were some of his best friends. Their family owned and operated Stargazer Ranch, and though Josh had been a couple years ahead of them at school, once he took over Split Valley, he'd become better acquainted with the brothers, frequently bumping into them at the feed store and at the Tenacity Social Club on his nights off.

"Is something wrong?" Noah asked. He crossed his arms, his flannel shirt bunching at his elbows. He looked tired, dark circles lingering beneath his eyes, though as a single dad to triplet toddlers, he always had that look about him. Between working the ranch and looking after his boys, Noah didn't have a lot of time for socializing, so Josh appreciated these visits even more. He also appreciated that they were willing to help out with a quick repair. It would save him from having to pull the ranch hands away from their work— he always employed a couple during calving season.

"Nothing's wrong," Josh assured him. "I'm just...thinking. That's all."

Ryder scoffed. "Thinking? In my experience," he said as he placed the toolbox in the bed of the truck, "only two things make a man sigh like that. Women and money. And I doubt the ranch is about to go under, so that only leaves one thing."

"Maybe those are the only two things you're thinking about," Noah said. Ryder was known for his roving eye. Josh was pretty sure he'd already dated every eligible woman in town.

"No," Ryder said, clapping Noah on the shoulder. "I also

think about how I can rile up my nephews right before bed-time."

"You're horrible."

"I keep things interesting." He climbed into the back seat of the truck.

Noah caught Josh's eye, shaking his head briefly. Josh closed the tailgate, then they both loaded up. Josh drove them down the long gravel drive toward the road, heading for the western border of his property.

"Okay," Ryder said. "Start talking. Who is she?"

Josh glanced in the rearview mirror. Ryder wore that cocky smile of his. The same one he used to woo the ladies in town. Luckily, they'd started getting wise to his tactics.

"It's no one."

"Sure," Ryder said.

Josh felt a flush creep up his neck. He might be the strong silent type, but he was usually pretty open with his friends. He just didn't know where to start. He'd spent all of fifteen minutes with Amy at the feed store yesterday, yet he couldn't seem to shake the thought of her.

Josh wasn't usually one to brood over women. He'd learned a long time ago that no good came from it. But there'd been a moment yesterday, while Amy was cashing him out, when he'd considered asking her out for coffee. He'd panicked, ob-viously, and turned tail, rushing out of the store as fast as he could. The problem was, he liked Amy, quite a bit. She'd been interesting and sweet, laughing at his pathetic jokes, and the words *cattle rancher* hadn't sent her running from him, unlike his past relationships. He just wasn't sure what to do about these feelings now. Despite wanting someone to share his life with, he'd come to the conclusion that looking for love only ended up with his heart stomped on. And he wasn't interested in living through that again.

"You know I've got a nose for these things," Ryder said. "I knew Renee and Miles had a thing before they even realized it. Trust me, I'll figure out who you've been talking to."

Noah and Ryder's sister, Renee, had recently found love with Miles Parker. But that's not what was going on here. "I haven't been talking to anyone," Josh said. "I talked. Singular. One time. To someone."

Ryder whooped from the back of the cab. "About time. You're getting as bad as Noah."

"I don't have time for dating drama," Noah said.

Josh glanced out the window, the fields rushing past. He thought he'd made his peace with his land and his cattle. But as much as he loved his work and the land, it was still a lonely existence, even for a man who had learned to enjoy the solitude.

"Okay, but who is she?" Ryder said.

"She's new in town." Josh's eyes lifted to the rearview again. "You don't know her."

Ryder's brow arched. "You sure?"

"Don't go getting any ideas." Josh slowed and drove onto the shoulder of the road, nearing the portion of downed fence. "Her name's Amy. She's working down at the Strom feed store."

"Aww, *Amy,*" Noah and Ryder chorused together.

"I hate you both." The truck bounced through some deep potholes, the supplies rattling around the bed of the truck, and the brothers broke into fits of laughter.

"Sorry," Noah said, trying to keep a straight face. "It was just the way you said it, all doe-eyed."

"Shut up."

"Tell us about Amy," Ryder interrupted.

"Nothing much to tell."

"Must be something to tell if she's got you this infatuated already," Noah pointed out.

Josh pulled up next to the fence. "I'm gonna make you both walk back to the ranch."

He got out of the truck. Noah and Ryder followed him to the back of the truck, unloading new fence posts and wire. "Can you blame us?" Noah asked, grabbing the tools. "How long's it been since you were last interested in someone?"

"A while," he muttered.

Honestly, it had been longer than Josh would care to admit. He wasn't a very exciting or adventurous man, and he liked his life the way it was. And that was maybe his downfall. When the woman he'd last seriously dated finally admitted she hated the idea of being trapped in this small town, in this world of ranchers and cattle, Josh had let her go without a fight. How could he possibly hold on to someone who wanted more out of life than what he could offer?

Now she was probably chasing rich cowboys across Montana. Which was for the best.

He turned his gaze to the property line. Split Valley stretched out before him in rolling pastures and meadows caught in a sea of sunlight. The cattle barn loomed like a dappled gray mountain, and the roof of his homestead rose up in two small peaks. Beyond that he could just make out the bulk of the herd, a mass of dark shadow, grazing in the farthest pasture. Maybe this was too simple of an existence for some people, but Josh never failed to be struck by its beauty.

"Give me a hand here," Ryder barked, breaking Josh from his thoughts.

He gathered up one side of the wooden post and helped Ryder carry it over to the fence, replacing the beam that had likely come down during a late winter storm. Noah brought over the toolbox and had a wheel of wire under his arm.

"Watch that there," Josh said, pointing out the rusty nails sticking out of the old beam. Ryder slipped on a pair of work gloves and dragged the old beam off to the bed of the truck.

As Josh set the new beam in place, his thoughts drifted back to his past. He worried now that a romantic partner was always going to expect more than he could provide. More adventure. More money. More thrilling things than what Tenacity had to offer. And as far as Josh went… He knew he was usually too quiet and too much of a homebody. He preferred the outdoors, getting mud on his boots in the pastures, to being cooped up in some stuffy building or surrounded by crowds of people. His social circle was small, and he liked it like that. Sure, maybe that all made him a bit boring, but was the idea of settling down with him that unfathomable?

"I think this'll hold," Noah said, packing earth around the base of the post. "Not going anywhere barring another wild storm."

"Hopefully we won't have to worry about one of those until the summer," Ryder said.

"Looks good," Josh agreed, giving the beam a shake. It held steady, so he released it, collecting supplies as Ryder and Noah strung new wire to keep the cattle contained. When they were finished and everything was packed back into the truck, they all climbed into the cab. Josh took the long way back to the ranch, doing a quick perimeter check, making sure no other posts had come down while he had Ryder and Noah with him.

"So… Amy," Noah said after a beat.

Josh laughed and shook his head. "There really is nothing to tell."

"Well," Ryder said, "maybe you should make a move and change that."

Josh hummed thoughtfully. Should he? Should he have

asked her for coffee? Or maybe to lunch? Would she have said yes?

"Look," Ryder said. "I know you love living in Lonely Valley, but it's okay to venture out of it every now and then. It's good for you even."

Josh snorted. Split Valley Ranch had earned its name from the small creek that crossed through the property, but in recent years Ryder had taken to calling it Lonely Valley or even Bachelor Island on occasion.

"I'm not the only one living in Lonely Valley right now," Josh said pointedly.

Ryder smirked. "I'm not lonely. Trust me. And Noah already has too many obligations to attend to. But you… You need this."

Josh reached the long gravel drive and drove them toward the house. Once they'd unloaded the truck, they relaxed in the chairs on the porch. Josh went inside to retrieve a couple of beers as a thank-you. When he returned to the porch, Noah looked up at him and said, "We think you should go for it."

"For what?"

"Amy."

"I barely know her," he said. He actually needed to get her off his mind.

Ryder reached for his beer. "That's the fun of it. Getting to know someone."

"Besides, what's the harm in asking her out?"

Josh could think of a lot of things. Maybe she'd flat out refuse. Maybe she'd agree and then realize he wasn't all that interesting. Would she though? She'd been surprisingly easy to talk to. He opened his beer and took a long sip.

"Remember what you said at the Fur-Ball?" Noah said.

He recalled the fundraiser for Loyal Companions, a local

animal rescue organization, but nothing else. "Not particularly. No."

"You said you weren't looking for Mrs. Right, just *Ms. Right Now*. Ring any bells?"

Josh shrugged. "Maybe."

"Exactly," Ryder cut in. "This doesn't have to be anything serious. Everyone deserves to have a little fun now and then. Even the president of Lonely Valley."

Josh snorted.

Noah shifted in his chair to face Josh. "Look, all I'm saying is if you feel like you hit it off with this woman, why not ask her out?"

"Because it'll probably end badly. So avoiding the whole thing seems wiser."

"Sure, if you never put yourself out there, you'll maybe save yourself the heartache, but you also might miss out on something really great."

Ryder laughed, almost choking on his beer. "Listen to the two of you, carrying on like the Quilting Club. Josh, you know what your problem is? You need to get laid and stop thinking so much."

"We can't all be a Lothario," Josh muttered.

Ryder grinned and nudged Josh's shoulder. "I'm serious. Every lady likes a grand gesture. Do something spontaneous, get her attention, and I'm telling you, she's yours."

"I don't know." The idea of doing anything particularly bold made him uncomfortable, especially without knowing if Amy was in any way interested.

"Better than you sitting around here moping with the cattle about it."

"I'm not moping."

"What would you call it then?"

"Look at it this way," Noah cut in. "If you don't ask her

out, Ryder will probably try. So just think of it like that. You're saving the girl from a far worse fate than you."

Josh burst into laughter as Ryder scowled at his brother. Noah spilled his beer down his shirt from snickering so hard.

In Josh's experience, telling himself not to think about something only made him want to dwell on it more. And he was beginning to think that he wasn't ever going to be able to shake Amy from his thoughts. He'd tried in a lot of ways since his conversation with Noah and Ryder a couple days ago. Really, he had. He'd thrown himself into his work. He'd gotten up earlier and went to bed later. He'd started projects he'd been putting off, and even made an effort to pop into the Tenacity Social Club to catch up with his neighbors.

The problem with ranching was it left him with a lot of time to think. Cattle weren't the best conversationalists, so his mind wandered. And no matter how often he redirected them, his thoughts inevitably returned to Amy.

His phone buzzed in his pocket, and Josh yanked it out, eager for the distraction. An image of his mother filled the screen. Josh answered it. "Hey, Mom. Thought you and Dad would already be on your way."

"Hi, honey. We just boarded the ship, but we don't depart for another couple of hours. They need time to get all the passengers and luggage on board. Can you believe your father almost misplaced his passport this morning?"

Josh checked his watch. Seattle was only an hour behind Tenacity. His parents would be destined for Alaska before lunch.

"Your father's disappeared in this breakfast buffet somewhere. I've never seen so much food. Harry!" she shouted suddenly. "Harry, get over here. Josh is on the phone!"

Josh laughed. He could just imagine his father heading

straight for an all-you-can-eat platter of bacon. His mother would be spending the entire trip hounding him about his cholesterol.

"Anyway," his mother continued. "We just wanted to check in before we left. I don't know when our next chance will be. I'm sure reception will be spotty once we're out at sea."

"Right."

"How are things going?"

"Good. The ranch is good. Calving season is on track."

"Mmm hmm," his mother said. "And is that all?"

"What are you talking about?"

"Don't pester the boy, Margaret," he heard his father say in the background.

"Quiet, Harry," his mother said. "I'm talking about this young lady that you've met."

Josh's jaw dropped. How the heck did she know about Amy all the way in Seattle? "I don't... I don't know—"

"Don't play that game with me, son."

"What game?"

"I spoke to Iris Strom. She mentioned that Faith said you'd been in the store, talking to some girl named Amy."

"Yes, because she works there." Josh sighed. Sometimes small towns were just too dang small. "She was helping me find the feed."

"Well, is she—" His mother cut off. "Oh, Josh, I have to go. Your father's found the bacon. Harry! Harold, that's enough."

He laughed. "Okay, Mom. You two have a good trip."

"I'll send you pictures. And don't think I've forgotten about this Amy person. I want to hear—"

"Think that reception's getting a little spotty, Mom."

"Nice try."

"I've gotta go. Love you." Josh hung up before his mother

could finish her sentence about Amy. There was nothing to tell, because they'd only had *one* conversation. And after the way things went with his last girlfriend, he didn't need to get his mother's hopes up.

Despite all that, Amy was still there, hanging out at the edge of his thoughts. Josh figured there was only one thing to do. He rushed through the rest of his chores and got into his truck, then drove down to Strom and Son Feed and Farm Supply.

He pulled into the parking lot, glancing at the front of the building.

What the hell was he doing?

Josh cut the ignition.

He hadn't driven all the way out here just because his mother had asked about Amy. Okay, not *just* because his mother had asked. It was because he didn't know how else to get her off his mind. That was the only reason. He needed to be able to focus on the ranch, and he couldn't do that if she kept popping into his thoughts.

Maybe Noah and Ryder were right. He should ask her out. What did he have to lose? His heart thumped in his chest. Putting himself out there again felt like a big step, one he didn't know if he was ready to take. But he'd already come this far. It would be ridiculous to turn back now without even trying.

Chapter Three

Amy stood on the top of a stepladder in the middle of aisle three, the back of her hand pressed to her lips as a wave of nausea as strong as an angry bull threatened to bowl her over. *Where the hell did this come from?* She didn't know if it was the lingering scent of hay that Caleb had just restocked in the warehouse or something on one of the shelves, but the cloying scent was turning her stomach like a blender. Amy clutched the shelf in front of her and took a deep, steadying breath.

She wasn't actually going to be sick, was she? Right here? In the middle of the store? She was too far away from the bathroom. She'd never make it. Her best bet would be to head for the trash can behind the cash desk but even that would be a risky dash.

Amy squeezed her eyes shut, willing everything in her stomach to settle. The nausea swept through her again, lingering on the back of her tongue, and she was almost afraid to swallow. Amy didn't often feel like this. The only time she did was during early morning rodeo training when she was doing a lot of activity and hadn't eaten enough.

And sure, maybe she'd skipped out on breakfast this morning. But who could blame her? Faith had been trying to stuff some turkey bacon-shaped something on a whole grain bagel in her hand, and that had sounded entirely unappealing. Though Amy usually turned her nose up at most of Faith's healthy choices—flax seed, quinoa, steel cut oats. It all just tasted like cardboard as far as Amy was concerned. Faith would have to pry real bacon out of her cold, dead hands. Amy had intended to grab breakfast when she got to the store. There was a cute little diner up the road that she'd been meaning to try for weeks, only she'd started stocking shelves and now it was almost lunchtime.

Still, this wasn't exactly the most arduous of tasks, and she'd skipped breakfast before, surviving on nothing but coffee and creamer. She shouldn't be feeling nauseated and slightly dizzy and tired.

Why was she so tired all of a sudden?

Amy fought off a yawn, worried that if she opened her mouth, it could be disastrous as far as the nausea was concerned. She clutched the shelf and took a short, even breath in through her nose. Then another. And another.

Slowly, the uncomfortable wave passed and Amy breathed easier.

There. All better.

She clearly needed to get some fresh air and some food into her. She'd no sooner thought about food than the nausea was back, so strong Amy clasped her hand over her mouth, certain she would be sick this time. *Okay, time to take a break*, she thought. From stocking. From the store. From the overwhelming scent of sickly-sweet hay. She just needed to get away from it all. But moving felt like a really bad idea.

What she needed was a distraction. Something to take her mind off the way her stomach was churning and bubbling, and the goose bumps that flushed down her arms, and the prickly heat that was suddenly creeping up her neck.

The bell over the front door jingled and Amy really hoped it wasn't a customer that was going to need her help. She didn't really feel like she was in any condition to be gathering up orders or showing people around.

"Well, look who it is!" Faith's voice soared over the sound of the bell, tinged with surprise. "Or should I say, look who the horse dragged in?"

"Sorry, I just came from the barn." That voice was familiar. Amy craned her head, looking down the aisle from the top of the stepladder. She couldn't quite see more than the corner of the cash desk. "I didn't even think about changing."

A figure stepped into view. Tall. Broad-shouldered. Long brown hair swept back, showing off a strong jawline. It was *him*.

Josh Aventura.

In the flesh.

Again.

The man her sister thought she should have asked out for coffee the other day. The man who she'd been thinking about nonstop since. It had been months since a man had occupied her waking thoughts. Certainly not since the early days of seeing Tru, and now in hindsight, he'd obviously been haunting her.

She tried to bite down on the smile that stretched across her face. She couldn't quite tell if she was thrilled to see him again, or if that was just the nausea, fluttering away in her chest. She reached onto the shelf and pulled a pallet of cans closer, facing the labels out to the front. What was Josh doing back here so soon anyway? Faith had said it would be close to a month before he'd be back for supplies. Perhaps he'd forgotten something.

Amy looked his way again.

She certainly hadn't forgotten how effortlessly handsome he was. It really was unfair for him to look that good after likely spending all morning with his cattle on his ranch.

He brushed at his shirt, knocking away dust.

"I'm kidding," Faith said. "I was just surprised to see you in here twice in one week. I'd say to what do we owe the pleasure? But usually when a customer returns that quickly it's with a complaint. Something wrong with the product we sold you?"

"No," Josh said, shaking his head. "No problem."

"So what? This just a social call?" Faith walked around the end of the cash desk, crossing her arms as she looked up at him. Her lips puckered, and Amy knew she was trying not to grin. "You checking up on your neighbors?"

"A man needs supplies," Josh said, so low Amy could barely hear him. His shoulders hunched up by his ears.

Faith threw her head back and laughed. "You know damn well we only see you in here once a month."

Josh dropped his hands to his hips. "Maybe I forgot a couple of things last time."

"Oh yeah? Like what?"

Amy shook her head. Poor Josh. She'd been on the wrong end of one of Faith's interrogations more times than she could count. If she wanted to know something desperately enough, Josh didn't stand a chance.

"Do you always harass your customers?" he asked gruffly.

"I'm not harassing, I'm showing a vested interest."

Josh reached out for one of the stands by the desk, pulling something from the display rack. He laid it on the desk.

"Wool sheep shears?" Faith said. "For a cattle ranch."

"Maybe I'm branching out," he said. "Or maybe I'm doing a favor for a neighbor. You want my money or not? Cause there's another perfectly good feed store up the road."

Amy smirked. Growing up on the rodeo circuit with a lot of sisters and cousins, Amy had quickly learned to compete with strong personalities. Josh might have been the gruff, quiet type who usually kept to himself, but Amy liked that he didn't take any of Faith's flak.

"Oh, I'll take your money," Faith said, clicking her tongue. "No need to act like you've got a burr in your saddle. I'm just saying… Sheep?"

"She giving you a hard time?" Caleb called, strutting across the store with Nathan and a pair of cowboy boot-clad ranchers in tow.

"Nothing I can't handle," Josh said.

Caleb slowed by the desk, leaning over to peck Faith on the cheek. He was incredibly tall, with deep brown skin, carved cheekbones, and an abundance of muscles from dragging around heavy bags of feed all day. Amy's heart swelled at the sight of them together. She really couldn't be happier that Faith had ended up with someone as kind and as doting as Caleb. Faith might give her a hard time, as sisters do, but she deserved all the happiness she'd found with Caleb.

"Be nice to the customers," Nathan called before carrying on. "I don't need them running off to the Feed and Seed."

Amy knew Nathan was joking. For as small as Tenacity was, with the sheer number of ranchers that lived and worked in the surrounding area, there was definitely a need for more than one feed store in town. Though each store still seemed to have their own loyal, longtime customers.

"I'm just reminding Mr. Aventura here that he runs a cattle ranch, not a sheep ranch."

Caleb hummed. "Maybe he's branching out."

Faith rolled her eyes so dramatically Amy could see it perfectly from where she stood. She muttered something that sounded like "*Men*," as Caleb wished Josh a good day and headed off after his father and the customers.

Faith turned her gaze back to Josh. "You want me to ring these shears up for you now?"

Josh turned, glancing around the store. "Not quite yet. I've got a couple other things to look for."

"Yeah, for that sheep ranch you're starting." Josh turned away from the counter, and Faith picked up the shears, placing them on the display shelf once more. She turned around and shot Amy a look, her lips curling into a smug smile.

Amy knew exactly what Faith was thinking, and resisted the urge to roll her own eyes at Faith's insinuation. She couldn't deny the fact that she was pleased to see Josh back in the store so soon, but it's not like he'd returned just to see her. He was a busy, hardworking man, and even if he didn't need sheep shears, they'd spent all of fifteen minutes together. Surely she hadn't made any type of worthwhile impression on the man.

He certainly made one on you though.

Amy pushed that thought aside. It disappeared quickly, lost in another wave of nausea, though this one was not nearly as bad as the first. She sucked in a sharp breath just as Josh's voice reached her.

"They pay you to stand around on top of stepladders all day?"

Amy turned her head. Josh had appeared from the other end of the aisle. He glanced up at her, the corner of his mouth lifting, a sack of feed tucked under one of his arms.

"Well, hello to you too, cowboy. I don't get paid at all, remember?"

"Ah, that's right." He took a step closer, and she could make out the way his brown eyes shone under the sunlight spilling in through the skylights. "You're just standing around out of the goodness of your heart."

"I am not *just* standing around," Amy scoffed. "I happen to be facing the product." She gestured down the aisle to all the cans she'd neatly arranged. "I'm even arranging it by expiration date."

"Oh, well, I'm sorry now for interrupting such vital work."

"You should be. I'm giving up my precious time to talk to you."

"Still haggling Caleb for employee of the month?"

Amy laughed. "As if there's any real competition. So, I hear you're branching out into sheep?"

"You do a lot of eavesdropping up there, huh?"

"Only on the interesting conversations. So, sheep?"

"What is it with you and Faith getting on my case about the sheep? Do I not look like I could handle some sheep?"

Amy's heart fluttered beneath her ribs. She suspected he hadn't really come to the store to secure supplies to start a sheep ranch. But before she could really wonder about what had brought Josh back so soon, a wave of dizziness consumed her. It started at the top of her head, like someone had cracked an egg right against her skull. The sensation slithered down her spine, rolling out across her body. She clutched the top of the stepladder as her head spun. This wasn't Josh having this effect on her, was it?

No, that would be ridiculous.

She didn't swoon over men.

Not even cowboys like Josh, who looked at her with big brown eyes and a smile that could knock the air right out of her lungs.

She'd learned her lesson.

Amy took a step down the ladder while she still had her balance. And another. She just had to get her feet back on solid ground. Then her stomach would settle and her head would stop spinning.

Right?

She reached up, palm to her forehead. Her mouth was dust dry. Her feet hit solid ground.

"Amy?" Josh said, his tone soft, concerned. She'd closed her eyes again so she couldn't see his face, but she felt his hand on her shoulder and that stirred more sensation in her gut. "You doing okay?"

"Fine," she squeaked in a voice that was too tiny to be her own. Then everything shifted sideways. Her head, her body... Her hip hit the stepladder, jostling it aside, and she was certain she was going to hit the floor next, but instead she crashed up against a wall of sturdy muscle.

Josh's arms wrapped around her upper arms, holding her upright with the kind of strength that would bruise, but Amy's other alternative was slumping straight to the floor. Her legs felt like sandbags, heavy and useless, and exhaustion surged through her, clinging to her bones.

"I don't think you're fine," he said. "You're the same color as my mother's china."

Oh, he was comparing her to porcelain. If she squinted maybe she could take that as a compliment. Porcelain was shiny and lustrous. Surely he didn't mean she was as pale and gaunt as she currently felt? One look at his face and she knew better.

"I really am fine," she insisted, trying to shake off the dizzy spell. Before she could, the nausea returned full force and Amy tried not to heave on Josh's boots.

"Okay," he said, sounding even more concerned. "Let's find you somewhere to sit down, huh?"

Amy let Josh guide her out of the aisle. She didn't have the strength to do anything else. She was like a rag doll in his arms.

"Faith!" he called. "Can I get some help?"

Amy heard panicked footsteps and Faith's sharp cry as she rushed over to meet them. "What happened?"

She took Amy by one arm, Josh kept to the other, and together they helped her into the chair behind the cash desk.

"What's going on?" Faith asked, pressing her hand to Amy's forehead the way their parents had when they were young. "You're not coming down with something, are you?"

"It's nothing," Amy said, shrugging her off. She didn't need Faith fussing over her like this. She especially didn't need her doing it in front of Josh. She'd practically already collapsed into the man's arms. That was enough mortification for one morning. "I got a bit dizzy coming down the ladder. That's all."

"It was a little more than nothing," Josh cut in.

"Dizzy?" Faith said. "Since when do you have a problem with heights?"

"I don't," Amy said. "It's probably because I didn't eat this morning." This was like trying to barrel race on an empty stomach with low blood sugar.

"You should have eaten that bagel I made you."

Amy wrinkled her nose as fatigue clung to her. She sighed. "I'm good now. I swear. I'll just get some food into me." She tried to stand, only to be hit with a shaky bout of weakness. Maybe she hadn't gotten enough sleep last night? That plus skipping breakfast might have been enough to make her feel like crap.

"I think I should take you home." Faith glanced up at the customers in the store. "Caleb should be finished with those ranchers soon. Do you think you can wait a little bit?"

Amy didn't want to admit it, but going home and crawling back into bed sounded like a dream. "I really am fine. I can drive myself back to your place. It's not that far."

"No!" Josh said at the same time Faith declared, "Absolutely not!"

Amy shrugged away from the force of their combined outburst. Faith's brows arched as she regarded Josh.

"I can drive you back to Faith's if you want," he said.

Faith's brows rose even higher, probably matching Amy's. "That's okay," she hurried to say. She'd already troubled him enough for one morning.

"You're sure it's no bother?" Faith said, completely ignoring Amy's huff of protest.

Josh shrugged. "Your place is on the way out to my ranch anyway. I'm driving by regardless."

Amy frowned. What was happening here? First of all, she was fine. Second of all, she was a big girl. She didn't need other people making decisions for her.

"You know what, that would actually be super helpful," Faith said. "Amy, I think you should take him up on his offer. You look like you're about to keel over."

"Gee, thanks," she muttered. But as much as she wanted to argue, to tell Josh and Faith exactly where they could stuff their good idea, she just didn't have the energy. Something had zapped it from her. "All right, fine. I'll take the lift."

"Great," Josh said. "I'll go pull my truck around front and be right back."

"Thanks again, Josh," Faith called after him.

The moment he was out the door, Amy's eyes cut across to Faith. "Don't do that," she all but hissed.

"Do what?" Faith asked, playing with the end of her long braid.

"Meddle."

"I don't know what you're talking about. I'm just trying to get you home safe and sound."

"By sending me off with a practical stranger?"

"Don't be ridiculous." Faith laughed. "Everyone knows everyone in Tenacity. And Josh wouldn't hurt a fly. You don't have to worry about him."

"The other day you said you'd barely ever heard the man speak more than a few words."

"Yes, in that gruff, stoic, lonely cowboy sort of way. Not in like a serial killer way."

Amy rolled her eyes. "Wonderful."

"You'll be fine. Seriously. But call me if you start to feel worse after he drops you off and I'll come home and take care of you."

Amy grumbled. She didn't need Faith to take care of her, and she especially didn't need her sister trying to set her up with a man while she was trying her best not to hurl all over the interior of his truck.

Chapter Four

"Stay put for a second. I'll give you a hand," Josh said as he pulled into the empty driveway at Faith and Caleb's place. A sun-bleached porch wrapped around the front of the property. It was a cozy, modern farmhouse filled with rustic country style. A wooden porch swing hung at one end of the house and two wooden rockers at the other. Vertical white siding covered the exterior of the house, stretching up to twin peaks with square windows. Amy thought it was the perfect little house in many ways. Right now it was perfect because her bed was just inside.

When Josh cut the ignition and the truck stopped rumbling, Amy felt like her insides were still shaking. Josh hopped out, hurrying around the front of the truck to collect her. He reached her door before Amy had even had a chance to open it.

"You don't have to escort me," she said as he swung the door open for her. "I'm perfectly capable of walking myself inside." She took a beat to make sure she was steady, then stepped out of the vehicle. It was a long way down and Josh caught her as she hit the ground. Amy resisted every urge to huff. She was not an invalid. And she'd only been a *little* dizzy. Now she had Josh tripping over himself to help her, and she felt silly. She also felt a little of something else as the heat of his hands pressed against her upper arms. Something that made her heart skitter in her chest. But she wasn't going to think about that or the flush that was creeping up her neck as Josh looked down at her, smiling a crooked smile.

Then he put a respectful bit of distance between them. "I don't mean to impose my help, but you do know that Faith will have my hide if I don't get you safely in the house, right?"

"What was that?" Amy said as an uncomfortable prickle of sensation washed through her. It wasn't quite dizziness, but it swept away her thoughts and made her stomach queasy. What the hell was going on? The feeling crept up on her, then receded, and she took an exaggerated breath, trying to get control of herself.

"Amy? You good? Not gonna hit the pavement on me, are you?"

The way he said her name sent a shiver through her—delight, maybe?—and Amy wanted to shake herself. *Get a grip, girl! He's just being friendly.* "I'm fine," she managed.

"You say that so often I'm starting to not believe you." He held out his arm to her. "I know you're insisting you don't need my help, but just humor me. Until we get you inside?"

Amy reached for him, latching onto his arm like one of those big suckerfish she and her sisters used to fish out of the river when they were young. She supposed this was the better alternative to fainting cold on the driveway. She had no doubt that Josh would catch her if she did in fact pass out, but how mortifying would that be? Then he'd have to drag her limp body inside while he called Faith and that was something she'd rather avoid.

"How're you doing?" Josh asked as they wandered up the driveway.

"Good."

"You don't sound very convincing."

Because with every step she felt like she was balancing on two spindles instead of legs.

"If it would make things easier I could just carry you inside."

Amy snapped her head up. "Don't you dare, Josh Aventura."

"Yikes! What'd I do to deserve the full name?"

"It's to let you know that I mean business."

"Noted." He pursed his lips and nodded. "Not a girl to be swept off her feet."

Amy snorted at that. After Tru, the last thing she wanted was someone swooping in and trying to dazzle her. Though she knew very well Josh had meant those words literally not figuratively. Amy doubted he had any plans to try and dazzle her. They still hardly knew each other.

"How about we agree to this then?" Josh said. "I will not offer to carry you unless there is an obvious threat to life or limb."

Amy leaned into the hold she still had on his arm. "I suppose that's reasonable. I don't think I'd be in any shape to refuse you in those particular circumstances."

"Glad you see it my way," Josh said. He looked over and she studied the way his hair parted, falling in soft waves on either side of his forehead. It was more than long enough to run her fingers through, and her mind wandered. She thought about the way it would feel to tangle her hands in it before she reeled herself in. She was already fighting dizziness, no need to make it any worse. His brown eyes studied her in return. Amy watched the way they crinkled, the lines by his eyes holding something like mischief.

Back at the store, Faith had given her the impression that Josh was a quiet man. The kind who kept to himself. But looking at him now, she was starting to think that Josh was anything but quiet. He expressed himself in a multitude of little ways—the curl of his smile, his narrowing gaze, the way he cocked his head at her, the way his thumb stroked her forearm. Amy thought Josh was saying an awful lot. Most people were probably just too busy to notice.

They reached the porch steps, and Amy thought Josh might leave her there, but he inclined his head toward the door. "We're going all the way," he said. "I don't intend to cross Faith."

"Probably for the best. You already had her in a fit over those sheep shears."

"Exactly. You wouldn't want me to face her wrath again so soon?"

"I see now why you offered to drive me. Trying to stay on her good side."

Josh looked over at her, his lips twisted. "I wasn't really after sheep shears," he admitted as they walked up the steps to the door.

"I figured," Amy said. She fumbled with her house key, finally getting it in the lock. "Seemed like a jump to go from cattle rancher to sheep rancher."

"Well, it's for the best probably. And I suppose I got what I wanted in the end anyway."

"But you left empty-handed."

"Not quite."

Amy's head snapped up, gazing into those brown eyes, and her breath caught. He couldn't mean… She stumbled against the doorframe. Great. Now she was dizzy all over again. There was no mistaking the fluttering in her chest this time. Nerves and adrenaline and excitement and… *Who are you to make me feel like this, Josh Aventura?*

He leaned toward her, huffing a laugh. "Thought you were perfectly fine."

Amy reached between them, turning the doorknob and shoving it open. "Might have spoken too soon."

"Where do you—" Josh started to say.

Amy pointed to the plush couch in the living room. It was soft fabric and swallowed her as Josh deposited her onto the cushions. She sank back with a heavy sigh.

"I think you're a little worse than you're letting on," Josh said.

"I'm really not," Amy tried to assure him. "It's just coming in waves. I'll be fine in a minute, after some rest." She touched the back of her hand to her forehead. Despite the weird cluster of symptoms, she really didn't feel sick. But she was clearly going to have to make sure she ate a proper breakfast in the mornings. She *was* getting older. Maybe her body was changing and telling her to take better care of herself. Maybe she was going to have to start eating Faith's turkey bacon. She wrinkled her nose.

Josh turned and headed for the door.

"Thank you!" Amy called after him, scrambling to sit up. "For the ride and for…well, everything." She wished she had the energy to work up more of a thank-you. She should at least offer him something to drink for his troubles, but she didn't have it in her. And that was a shame because she really liked talking to Josh. Amy ran a hand through her hair. Damn Faith and her need to interfere. She hadn't even gotten around to asking Josh out for coffee yet, and after today she wasn't sure she ever would.

He'd obviously had more than enough of her. Probably couldn't wait to get back in his truck and flee to his ranch.

She heard the door close, but to her surprise, Josh was still standing there. *Oh.* He toed out of his boots, then turned to face her. "Where's the kitchen?" he asked, lifting his hand to gesture down the hall. "Through here?"

Oh! Amy propped herself up a little more. She could do this. If Josh wanted to stay a minute, she could rally. "Would you like something to drink? Can I get you—"

Josh was by her side in an instant, settling her back into the cushions. He wedged one of Faith's fancy, frilly pillows behind her back. "Don't get up," he said. "Just make yourself comfortable."

Amy smirked up at him. He was so close she could count the dark stubble on his cheeks and chin. "I think you stole my line."

The corner of his mouth twitched. "You might be surprised to hear it, but I actually know my way around a kitchen pretty well. And before I go, you at least need some water. Maybe you're just dehydrated."

"Josh, I can get it. Really. Please don't trouble yourself."

"Sit," he said in that gruff way of his. It sounded like an order. "I won't take any arguing."

Amy frowned after him as he made his way to the kitchen. She felt odd, having Josh wait on her in Faith's house, but she didn't want to offend him after he'd gone out of his way to help her. Plus, a silly little part of her liked that she got to indulge in his company for a little while longer. She sank back, listening to cupboard doors open and close. She could hear him puttering around, shifting glasses, and then the squeak of the sink tap. When he returned to the living room, he had a tall glass of water in his hand.

"Drink," he said as he handed it to her.

"Is that another order?"

"A strong suggestion."

Amy took a sip. It was refreshing, but she wasn't parched, so she doubted her dizzy spell had anything to do with being dehydrated. "Thank you," she said anyway. "For this. For driving me home."

He studied her again with those deep brown eyes, and Amy felt her cheeks flush. She didn't know why, but under the strength of his gaze, she felt oddly cared for.

"You need something to eat," he finally said. "How about some toast and sweet tea?"

"The water is plenty," she said, but he was already making his way back to the kitchen.

"I assume you *like* toast?"

"Who doesn't like toast?" she called.

"According to my grandmother," Josh said, his voice carrying across the house, "a good piece of toast could settle your stomach and all your woes."

"She sounds like a wise lady."

"She was. She also used to keep sweets in her purse for whenever she visited the ranch. Some for me. Some for the horses."

Amy came from a long line of strong, stubborn women—especially her mother and grandmother—so she could appreciate how fondly Josh spoke of his grandmother. She closed her eyes briefly, listening to the sounds of Josh moving about the kitchen. She imagined him at the counter, strong shoulders, perfectly parted hair, those forearms... The toaster popped and her eyes flew open. Heat pooled in her chest. Maybe it was better not to be imagining those sorts of things.

Josh returned a few minutes later with some buttered toast and sweet tea. He handed it to her, and Amy sat up. "Looks like the color is starting to come back to your cheeks," he noted.

That only made Amy flush harder. The color was back for all the wrong reasons. "I think I'm feeling much better. You don't have to stay."

"Right," Josh said, giving her a curt nod. "I'm glad to hear it."

Amy felt the energy in the room shift as Josh turned toward the door.

"Wait," Amy said suddenly. "I'm sorry, that felt abrupt. I didn't mean to rush you out, especially after you were kind enough to make me something to eat. I hope you didn't think that." She was messing up this entire thing.

"I didn't think that," Josh said. "But I'm also not trying to overstay my welcome."

"You're not," Amy said. "It's not that I want you to leave. I just figured you probably had more important things to be getting on with. I'm sure the ranch needs your attention."

He shrugged. "Well, even if I do, I'm still happy to sit a spell with you. If that's something you'd like, of course."

Yes! she wanted to shout. *Stay for a spell. Stay with me.* She didn't want this to end just yet. "I would like that very much." His face lit up at her words. "How about we sit on the porch though? I think I could use a bit of fresh air again."

"Sounds good." Josh helped her up and carried her sweet tea and toast out to the porch.

Amy settled into one of the wooden rockers. The day was sunny, the air cool but not chilly. She let the energy settle into her, let it wash away her earlier dizziness. She felt better out here with the endless blue sky stretching across town. It was the perfect kind of day, actually, made all the better by the fact Josh was here.

The fact that he wanted to be here was something Amy was still trying to wrap her head around.

"Can I get you anything else?" Josh asked.

"No, but will you at least get yourself a drink? I'm feeling like a terrible host."

"Please don't," Josh said. "We're here because you weren't feeling well, not so you could wait on me."

Amy smiled up at him. "Just get some sweet tea, please?"

"If it'll stop you from stressing."

"It will."

He disappeared into the house again. While he was gone, Amy picked away at her toast, even the crusts, which she usually left behind, finding herself ravenous. When had buttered toast ever tasted so wonderful? Josh returned with a glass in hand.

"Happy now?" he asked, plopping down in the rocker next to hers. He kicked his legs out, the toes of his boots worn and dusty.

"Yes," Amy said, grinning. Caleb and Faith often sat out here like this in the evenings, after the store was closed and dinner was cleaned up. More than once, Amy had thought about how lovely it must feel to sit in the quiet company of someone you cared about. "So, do you get any time to do this out on that ranch of yours? Or is it just work, work, work all the time?"

"You know, I usually put the cattle in charge and they take care of things for me."

"Oh, of course. I'm sure they're running the ranch right now."

"Keeping it in top shape," Josh agreed.

"No, but really?" Amy said.

"I mean, do I kick back on the porch and relax? On occasion. Usually only if I have people stop by for whatever reason. When it's just me, I usually have a running list of things that need to get done around the property and I just fill my time. It's the kind of job where you're never really caught up, if that makes sense. There's always some wayward cow getting stuck in the creek or some storm tearing down fences or supplies that need to be gathered."

Amy nodded. "I guess you could say *I'm* the one doing *you* the favor. Forcing you to relax in the middle of the day."

Josh sipped his sweet tea, hiding his smirk. "This was all for my benefit then?"

"It's looking that way."

"I see. Guess I should be thanking you."

"It's the least you could do," Amy said. "After the big show I had to put on to get you here."

Josh chuckled. "I am glad you seem to be feeling better."

"The toast worked wonders."

"Now that's a best kept secret, so don't go spreading it around."

"Oh, I would never." Amy pretended to lock her lips and toss the key away. She glanced back at him. "Tell me about Split Valley."

"What do you want to know?"

"Tell me about the horses. You said you have a few?"

"Well," Josh said, "There's Bella and Bitsy. I've had Bella since I was a teen. She's older and grumpy now, but still my best girl. Bitsy likes who she likes and bites everyone else. But we're working on it."

Amy laughed. "Sounds like quite the character."

"Oh, she is. And then there's Mac. Short for Macbeth, because he's just full of drama. But he's also very sweet and gentle, and as long as I sneak him a treat every now and then, I can usually get him to keep the melodrama to a minimum."

Amy loved the way he talked about his horses. There was warmth and affection, and she very much wanted to meet this little herd. His voice was soothing as he carried on about their personalities, about Bitsy not being allowed near visitors, about the oddball things that horses do. Amy could have listened to him talk all day about everything and nothing. As it was, everything sounded so much more interesting. He could have been telling her about the clouds in the sky and she suspected she'd still be hanging on every word.

"So how long have you been riding?" Josh said. "You mentioned it the other day at the store that it's one of your favorite things."

"I started learning… Gosh, I must have been three or four," Amy said. "But I'd been around horses my whole life." She glossed over The Hawkins Sisters stuff again because she wanted Josh to know her without all the glitz and glam.

"Did you get yourself a tiny little pony?"

"That's exactly what I had!" Amy laughed. "Me and all my sisters. We used to fight over who got in the saddle first."

"I'm trying to imagine a tiny you, kicking up dust and wrinkling your nose when you didn't get your way."

"I try not to scrap with my sisters anymore," Amy said. "I don't think I ever outgrew the nose wrinkle though."

"It's okay." The corner of his mouth quirked in that half smile. "It's cute."

Amy chased away her blush with a huge gulp of sweet tea. Josh either didn't seem to notice, or politely chose to ignore her, carrying on the conversation. They kept talking and before Amy knew it, over an hour had passed and Josh showed no sign of leaving.

Amy basked in the perfection of the weather and his company. In the back of her mind, though, a small, annoying thought couldn't help drawing her attention to Tru. He had seemed sweet too, once upon a time, and she'd foolishly trusted that sweetness.

When she'd met Tru last October at the Golden Buckle Rodeo held at the Bronco Convention Center, Amy had thought he was something special. He was the kind of person who gave you his full attention when you talked, making you feel like you were the only person in the room. And when he'd singled her out for conversation, Amy was not only flattered but shocked, falling for those false charms so fast she was surprised she didn't land flat on her face.

Josh seemed different in so many ways. In all the ways that mattered, perhaps. But her heart skipped for him the way it had once raced for Tru, and that made her nervous. Still, she tried to imagine Tru dropping everything, putting his entire day on hold, just to take care of her the way Josh had today, and she couldn't—so that had to mean something. Didn't it?

Amy pushed the thoughts from her mind, determined to enjoy what was left of their afternoon together. Only when Josh left, did Amy realize how refreshed she felt. It was almost as if Josh had lifted some sort of darkness off her, and that was certainly more than she could ever say about Tru McCoy.

Chapter Five

"It's not weird," Josh said to Bella as he removed her tack, tossing the heavy saddle over the gate. He picked up a brush and swept it across her broad back, her roan coat gleaming in the early morning sun that spilled in through the barn door. "I'm just gonna swing by and see how she's feeling after yesterday."

Bella snorted, the sound muffled with her face in her feed bucket.

Josh had a habit of talking to his horses. He hadn't noticed until one of his hired hands pointed it out one day, and they'd all had a good laugh about it. Josh supposed he talked to most of his animals. He spent a lot of solitary time out here, with nothing but the cattle and the horses as company, so some one-sided conversation was expected. Besides, the horses never complained. As long as he bribed them with a bucket of oats and a thorough brushing, they were content to listen as long as he needed.

"It's the neighborly thing to do," he continued. "I know we're not *technically* neighbors, but it'd be rude of me not to inquire. Wouldn't it? I mean, I use the feed store every month. Don't you think it would be weird *not* to say something?"

Bella's ear twitched.

"That's not particularly helpful," Josh said, giving Bella a firm pat.

He'd been thinking about Amy since the moment he'd gotten up this morning, wondering how she was faring, if she was feeling any better, if she'd be back at work today. He tried to tell himself it was just genuine concern, but a small part of him knew it was more than that.

He'd spent the better part of yesterday afternoon with her, sitting out on the porch, and Josh honestly couldn't remember when he'd enjoyed himself more. It had been a perfect spring day, but the truth was that it was the company that had been so pleasant. It could have been blowin' up a storm and he'd still have enjoyed himself just the same. Frankly, Amy was the only thing occupying his thoughts, and he'd come to the conclusion that the only way to stop said thoughts was to see her again. When he'd left her yesterday, the color had come back to her cheeks and she laughed freely at the stories he told her about wayward cattle on the ranch.

But he couldn't shake the desire to see her again. To make sure she really was feeling better.

"It's not weird," he said again as he locked Bella's stall and hung up the tack.

It was perfectly normal to be concerned about a neighbor. A charming, sweet, interesting neighbor. Not to mention beautiful. Because he'd be lying to himself if he didn't acknowledge the way Amy's pretty smile, directed right at him, made his pulse skip like a frog into a creek bed.

He thought again about what Ryder and Noah had said the day they'd visited. *Go for it.*

And why the hell not? Josh asked himself. They'd had a good time yesterday—him and Amy—after she was feeling a little better. Perhaps they'd have an even better time if he worked up the nerve to ask her to lunch.

Because it's going to hurt, a voice whispered inside his head. *It's going to get messy and she'll stomp all over your heart.*

Hush, he wanted to tell the voice. He glanced at his watch. If he was going to check up on Amy and maybe catch her before lunch, he had to go now. Josh darted inside to change out of his dusty riding clothes. He wetted his hands and ran them through his hair, making sure everything lay flat before he hurried back out to his truck. The quicker he went, the less time there was for him to talk himself out of this idea.

Josh followed the long gravel drive out to the main road, passing the sign for Split Valley that sat carved in thick, polished wood next to the entrance of the property. Growing up on Juniper Road, Josh had watched ranches come and go, most falling on hard times. There were few that had endured the economic hardship Tenacity had been plagued with. But there were acres of land to the west of the Split Valley that belonged to the Coreys. Josh had always been close to them, having practically grown up with their grandson, Shane. And to the east was the property that had once belonged to the Woodsons. Fences lined the road, wood and wire and steel, keeping the animals contained and marking out property lines. At this time of year, the first wildflower blooms were stretching out of the ditches in thick clumps.

Josh had always appreciated growing up out here, just beyond town. Out where the world quietly shifted from one season to the next. And though he'd come to appreciate that reliable change from winter to spring, he sometimes thought it might be nice to have someone in the passenger seat to enjoy it with him.

He reached town after another minute, his truck trundling along Central Avenue. He passed The Grizzly Bar with its weather-beaten benches and large orange door. Next door was the Silver Spur Café where Josh had spent a good many mornings enjoying coffee and eggs. Town Hall rose up right in the middle of everything, that old busted clock tower looking out over the town. Then there was Tenacity Drugs & Sundries, and the Tenacity Social Club, built in the basement of the same building that housed their post office and barbershop. The businesses that survived in this hard-scrabble town did so out of pure grit and determination. He drove past the Feed and Seed and a while later pulled into the parking lot of Strom and Son.

Josh hopped out of his truck and quickly checked his hair in the reflection of the window, then walked into the store.

He nodded to Nathan as he passed by with a box of nutritional supplements and spotted Faith at the front counter. She glanced up, and her eyes narrowed slightly, the corners of her mouth quirking.

"You again?" She placed a hand on her hip. "Here for more sheep shears?"

Josh clicked his tongue. Faith was far too astute for her own good. No point in lying. He leaned against the counter. "I actually just wanted to see how Amy was getting on after yesterday."

"Huh," Faith said. "Did you?"

Her gaze almost made him squirm. Maybe he should have stuck with the lie.

"Well, I suppose you could ask her yourself," Faith said. She inclined her head in the direction of the warehouse. "Amy's out back."

"Right," Josh said. "Thanks."

He could feel Faith's eyes on him until he passed through a door and out of sight, disappearing into a back lot where a supply delivery was being unloaded from a large box truck. He spotted Amy right away, her dark hair hanging just past her shoulders, tapping a pen against her chin. She had a clipboard in hand and her lips moved like she was counting under her breath.

He cleared his throat as he approached so he didn't startle her.

Amy's eyes widened. He hoped it was a good surprise. Then her face broke into a smile. "Well, hey there, cowboy."

He liked the way she called him *cowboy*. He liked it too much, probably.

"I didn't think I'd see you again so soon."

"Hope I'm not interrupting anything," Josh said. "I sort of just wanted to check in and see how you were doing."

Amy flushed. "I'm actually feeling much better," she said, tucking the clipboard under her arm. "And Faith wouldn't let me leave the house this morning until I'd eaten a turkey bacon sandwich. So no spontaneous fits of dizziness either."

"Turkey bacon?"

"I've been trying to sneak real bacon into the house since I got here back in February. Faith won't budge."

"Wow, you really are suffering."

"Thank you," Amy said. "No one else seems to understand my plight."

"Really though, I don't know how you can bear it."

Amy laughed, and he caught a flash of teeth. She did look better. Brighter. Glowing even. It was such a sharp contrast to yesterday that Josh actually sighed, relief washing through him. He knew he'd been worried, he just hadn't realized *how* worried. "I'm glad you're feeling better."

"Well, I've also been keeping up with my sweet tea and toast," she said. "And it's been working wonders."

He chuckled under his breath, charmed that she remembered what he'd said about his grandmother.

"You didn't come all the way here just to check up on me, did you?"

"I might have."

Amy ducked her head, her hair obscuring the deepening flush in her cheeks. She held the clipboard to her front, like it might stop his words from reaching her. "You really didn't have to do that. Your help yesterday was more than enough."

"I know." Josh shrugged. "But I wanted to." And he wanted to keep talking to her. Even now. "Is it busy today?" He gestured to the skids of supplies. "I mean, do you still have a lot of work to be getting on with here?"

Amy glanced. "Not too much more actually. I was almost done when you turned up."

"You think you could leave for a bit?"

She arched her brow.

"For lunch," he clarified.

"Are you asking me out for lunch, Josh Aventura?"

"If that's something you'd be open to," he said. "If you're not, then I will just be on my way. And we can both pretend I was never here asking awkward questions." He started to back away but she caught him by the wrist. Warmth flooded through him at the touch.

"I'd love to go to lunch with you," she said sweetly, and Josh's heart lobbed against his ribs. It was so forceful he worried she might be able to see it beating right through his shirt.

"Great. That's really... Okay then." He waited for Amy to finish up her counting, then they headed back through the store together. Amy stopped briefly to speak with Faith who was eyeballing him over Amy's shoulder, her eyebrows rising higher and higher. Josh wasn't sure what that look meant, but he averted his eyes just in case.

When their conversation was finished, Amy followed him out to his truck and he drove them back down Central Avenue to the Silver Spur Café. They'd just missed the lunch rush, which meant it would be quiet inside, but they should still have enough time to eat before the café closed for the day.

"How's this?" Josh asked as he stopped in the parking lot. There weren't a plethora of options in Tenacity, but he could vouch that the food was good. Definitely not a five-star experience. It actually might not even compare to what she was probably used to having up in Bronco. But the owners were kind, and he'd never once heard a bad word about the service. "I know it's not much," he continued. Damn. Maybe he should have planned this out more. It was his first time asking her out. Should he have sprung for something better? Should he have cooked?

"This is perfect," Amy said. "I'd been meaning to check it out, just hadn't gotten around to it yet."

Josh nodded and took his keys from the ignition, emboldened by Amy's words.

They walked inside, greeted by cozy booths and wooden tables and an eclectic mix of cowboy paraphernalia tacked to the wooden ceiling beams. There were photos of people from town in frames adorning the walls behind the hostess stand. Ranches and ranchers. Young couples and old. Newly married folks and babies. It summed up Tenacity pretty well.

"Cute," Amy said, studying one of the photos.

They were seated quickly, and he briefly glanced at the menu, but put it aside knowing he was going to order his favorite. The brisket burger.

"There are too many options," Amy laughed, lowering her menu. Her blue eyes twinkled in the low light overhead.

"What have you narrowed it down to?"

"Maybe the chicken club with the pickle spears on the side."

"Good choice."

Their waitress came over and talked Amy into also getting their homemade soup. When their food arrived, he was pleased to see Amy eating with gusto, again reassured that she really was feeling better.

"So, is this place like a Tenacity staple?" Amy asked, studying the photos on the walls again. "Been around since the beginning of time sort of thing?"

"I've actually been coming here since I was a kid," Josh said. "I've lived in Tenacity my whole life. Never left town. So it's been around at least that long."

"Not for college or anything?"

"No, I took over the ranch from my parents in my early twenties."

"And you never wanted to leave?"

He shook his head. "This place might not work for some people. But I've always been content with what the world had to offer me right here." Though, of course, a nice woman, a partner in this life, could only make it better, but Josh had come to the conclusion that that ship had probably sailed. Still, with Amy sitting across from him it was easier to dream of a future that looked like that. "What about you? Get out of Bronco much?"

"Actually," she said, wiping her hands on a napkin and giving him a sheepish little smile. "I've done a lot of traveling with my family. Like an exorbitant amount. For work mostly."

"So, you're not really a feed store shelf stocker?" he teased.

"No, I'm…actually in the rodeo business like Faith."

"Wait! I knew Faith was one of The Hawkins Sisters, but I didn't realize you were also one of *those* Hawkinses." He tipped his head, staring like he was seeing her for the first time. He'd seen dozens of posters promoting local rodeo events, highlighting The Hawkins Sisters with their rhinestone cowboy hats and lassos. But even knowing Faith's connection to the rodeo, he'd never once considered that Amy might also be involved. It seemed so obvious now. "I don't know how I didn't put two and two together." It was literally in the name. The Hawkins *Sisters*.

"Yeah. I'm sorry I didn't mention it before. I just… When I bump into people that's usually the first thing they bring up. And if they're rodeo fans, they want pictures and autographs. But you didn't say anything, and at first I just thought you were being nice. But then I actually wondered if you really didn't know who I was. You just seemed to see *me,* without the name and the family and the fancy rope tricks. And I kind of wanted to keep existing in that bubble for a minute."

"I really had no idea," he said. "I feel kind of like an idiot now."

"Don't," Amy said. "Please. It was my choice not to tell you."

Josh watched her wring her hands together. He hadn't meant to make her uncomfortable. "If you don't want to talk about it, we don't have to. I can steer clear of the conversation."

"Oh, it's nothing like that. I love my family. Don't get me wrong. But sometimes it's nice just to get to be Amy, if you know what I mean?"

"Sure."

"But I don't mind talking about it."

"So… A Hawkins Sister. That's…wow." He was impressed not only by her rodeo prowess, but also by her worldliness. With his ranching responsibilities, he'd never been able to travel far. In fact, he might even be a little intimidated by how vastly different their worlds now felt. But he really did like her, and Amy genuinely seemed interested in him, so he tried not to dwell on how his simple life could possibly measure up to hers. "You said you did a lot of traveling?"

Amy nodded. "Faith and I and one of our sisters Tori spent a lot of time in South America during our last rodeo tour. Our other sisters Elizabeth and Carly were in Australia with some of the Hawkins cousins. So, you know," she laughed, "we get around."

"Which of all your trips was your favorite?"

"Definitely a show we did down in São Paulo, Brazil, near a community called Barretos where they have this local cowboy festival. They were just so excited to have us there and the crowds had so much energy. There's just something about when the crowd is excited and your heart is beating and you can feel the power of the horse beneath you. Really makes me remember why I love it so much."

To Josh it all sounded exciting and glamorous, and though he knew he could never compete with all that adventure, he was intrigued by her stories. "São Paulo is a long way from Tenacity. A different world entirely." He chuckled and said, "Probably much more charming, too."

"Oh, I don't know about that," Amy insisted. "Tenacity has its charms, I think."

He guffawed. No one had ever called Tenacity charming before, at least as far as he'd heard, and he was tickled that she would say that.

"I think it's mostly just that I've had my fill of big cities," Amy said. "For a long time the circuit and the travel and the performing was what I thought I wanted."

"Not so much anymore?"

She shrugged, her nose wrinkling in that adorable way. "I think some peace and quiet would be nice now. Tenacity seems like the perfect place for that."

Josh nodded. "A person can find peace here," he agreed. "But it can also be lonely sometimes."

Her smile thinned. "I've come to understand a thing or two about loneliness recently."

Her words were soft and sad, and Josh reached over to take her hand, to comfort her, but before he could, Amy flinched away, and he felt like an idiot. Lord, what was he doing? "I'm sorry." He cleared his throat. "I didn't mean to be so forward." Maybe he was reading things wrong and Amy was only humoring him with lunch. With conversations on the porch. With sweet smiles and pink cheeks and... Before he could fret anymore about overstepping, Amy shook her head.

"No. I'm the one who should apologize." She frowned. "It's just, I've recently gotten out of a bad relationship and I guess I'm just a little cautious."

Josh nodded. "Of course. No need to apologize."

They went back to eating.

"I really am glad you asked me to lunch," she said.

"Yeah?"

Amy nodded. "Yeah."

"Good," he said softly, and for the life of him, Josh couldn't figure out who had been foolish enough to let Amy get away.

Chapter Six

Josh turned into the Strom and Son parking lot without really thinking about it.

He'd been to the post office to check up on a package, and seeing the feed store, his thoughts had immediately turned to Amy, and before he knew it, he was parked and walking through the door.

There was a bounce to his step and a giddy flutter in his chest as he stepped inside. When had this become his favorite spot in Tenacity?

"Welcome to Strom and Son," he heard. "How can I—" Faith popped out of an aisle, took one look at him, and grumbled. "We're gonna have to put a bell on you so I stop wasting my breath. Amy's in the office."

"Would she mind some company?"

"Well, why don't you ask her and find out." Faith shot him a funny little smile before wandering off.

Well then, Josh thought. Faith might like to pretend that seeing him here was a nuisance but she also seemed to be going out of her way to encourage…whatever this was.

What was this?

He headed for the back office. The door was ajar, the sign posted said EMPLOYEES ONLY. He obviously liked Amy's company. His mother would call him smitten.

Noah and Ryder would say he had a crush.

But the word *crush* didn't feel quite right, he decided, as he knocked, peeked inside and spotted Amy. The sight of her smile stole his breath away. It was somehow more than just a simple crush, and that thought made him feel ridiculous. Like he'd jumped into a rodeo ring without ever having learned how to ride a horse first. He felt like he'd skipped some crucial steps somewhere. And yet explaining away his feelings as a simple crush wasn't possible.

He liked Amy Hawkins.

That much was true.

But he liked her in a way that didn't make sense to him.

It was too much, too fast.

Only he didn't know how to undo it. *Take it slow*, he told himself. *Don't jump into this.* Problem was he'd already taken a running leap off the diving board.

She sat in a chair behind a long, wooden desk, holding a granola bar. There was an uneaten apple on the desk. "Hey there, cowboy."

He leaned against the doorframe. "Not interrupting anything, am I?"

"No." Amy gestured with her granola bar. "It's my new mandatory snack break." Her lips quirked at the corners. "Faith's been on me since the other day."

"That doesn't surprise me. She seems like a stickler for that sort of thing."

"She worries too much."

"Because she cares?"

"Remains to be seen," Amy joked. "So back for more—"

"If that sentence ends in sheep shears you might want to rethink it."

Amy's eyebrow arched dramatically. "Careful, cowboy.

If you keep swinging by like this for no reason I might start to think you *want* to see me."

He huffed. This woman knew damn well he wanted to see her. "Maybe I do."

Amy hummed thoughtfully. "Can't imagine why."

"Isn't it obvious?"

She shrugged.

"If I get in good with Faith's sister I might qualify for the friends and family discount."

Amy guffawed. "Oh, of course. I'm on to your schemes now."

"Good."

"You know, you're less charming when I know you're just using me for your own personal gain."

Josh crossed his arms and cocked his head. "Huh."

"What?"

"You think I'm charming."

Amy flushed like she was only now just realizing what she'd said. "Past tense," she muttered. "You *were*."

"I don't think that matters." He stared at her, and he swore the flush spread down her cheeks to her throat. A place he'd very much like to press his lips. He wanted to see if her pulse fluttered under his kiss. He wanted to—

"Well, I also think puppies are charming and seniors that sing in barbershop quartets. So don't let it go to your head. Might not be able to get your cowboy hat on anymore."

"Worried about my ego?"

"Yes. With that head of hair you don't have much room to work with."

So she thought he was charming and had good hair? If he was ever in need of a compliment he knew where to come. She met his eye and held his gaze for a long moment. "I didn't just come here to get my ego stroked."

"No?"

"I actually swung by because I was wondering… I mean, I had a really nice time the other day. At lunch."

Something about her softened, and Josh wanted to sweep her into his arms. "I did too," she said.

He nodded. Reassured. "Good. Great." He cleared his throat. "I thought maybe you'd like to go for a ride then? Up at my ranch. We could take the horses out, I could show you the property. It's a nice, easy trail. Though I suppose you're not one to shy away from some rough terrain."

Amy lit up. "I'd love that actually."

"Perfect," Josh said. If he'd known that, he wouldn't have taken so long to spit it out. "I guess I'll pick you up later? At Faith's?"

"Sure."

He smiled, backing away from the doorway. "See you then."

"See you, cowboy."

Josh turned, heading for the exit, practically buzzing with energy. He clapped a surprised Caleb on the shoulder as he passed him. "Hey, man. How's it going?"

"Hey?" Caleb said.

Josh was out the door before he could say any more. The faster he got back to the ranch and finished up with the chores, the faster he could get back to Amy.

Josh pulled into Caleb and Faith's driveway several hours later. He'd run later than planned, thanks to a complicated calf birth that required a call to the local large animal vet. But as Josh's father used to say, mother nature changed her plans for no one, so he'd texted Amy, telling her he was absolutely still coming to pick her up, just a little later than anticipated.

There was still enough time left in the day for a ride, plus if the weather cooperated, it should make for a pretty decent sunset. And who didn't like a nice sunset?

When Amy appeared on the porch, Josh got out to meet her.

She wore jeans, a jewel-toned plaid shirt, and a black puffer vest. It wasn't exactly cold, but at this time of year the temperature did drop the closer it got to sundown. Her hair was pulled back too, tied off in a high ponytail, and he admired the long, graceful line of her neck as she came down the steps.

"How are mother and baby?" she asked.

"Everyone's doing well. Doc said there should be no issues going forward."

She grinned at that and he walked her around to the passenger side of the truck, opening the door for her. "You didn't have to get out," she said, giving him a look that was both amused and a little exasperated. "I am fully capable of opening my own door."

He leaned against the open door. "I know that, but I wanted to."

"Well, just don't expect any more ego stroking."

"I would never." He grinned at her, already basking in the pleasure of her company.

"So, are we gonna go ride some horses?" she said. "Or are you gonna stand there and keep staring at me?"

Josh laughed. He liked how cheeky she could be. How bold. "What would you say if I decided I just wanted to keep staring?"

"Hmm. You're not supposed to ask that question." She reached out, nudged him out of the way and closed the door.

Josh rounded the front of the cab and climbed into the truck, starting the ignition. "But I did ask," he said, backing out of the driveway.

"Then I would say you're wasting precious horseback riding time."

"I don't think any time with you is ever wasted."

Amy opened her mouth. Closed it. Her cheeks pinked. "Just drive, cowboy."

"Did your words get tangled?"

She snorted.

"I mean it, you know. If you didn't want to come to the ranch, I would have done anything else. I just…wanted to spend some more time with you."

"And I wanted to spend time with your horses."

He barked a laugh. "Glad we cleared that up."

They grinned at each other again as Josh went racing down Juniper Road to the ranch, the fields on either side of them painted a soft green in the late afternoon sun. He'd driven this road thousands of times, but now he wondered what Amy saw when she looked at it. Did she think the fields looked like rolling green waves? Could she smell the honey-suckle that wafted from the meadows? Could she hear the buzz of insects on the wind?

"How was the rest of your day?" he asked.

"Well, Faith put me to work discounting old stock."

"Fascinating."

"I know. I'm allowed to put big yellow stickers on everything I can reach from the ground." Amy huffed. "I think since the other day she's afraid to let me near a ladder or lift anything heavy."

"Have you been feeling poorly again?" Josh asked, suddenly worried.

"No, I've felt fine. She's just…overprotective sometimes. Sisters, you know."

He tilted his head thoughtfully. "Wouldn't know. I'm an only child."

"Oh," Amy said. "I guess it's like… When you're young, you affectionately want to kill your siblings all the time. For everything. Stealing your clothes. Breathing too loud. Eating your food. Talking to the boy you like. And then you sort of, I don't know, grow up a bit. And you hit this place where they're suddenly your best friends and you'd do anything for them. Fight off the world if you had to." She laughed to herself. "It probably sounds strange."

"No," Josh said. "It sounds…nice." He didn't know what it was to have siblings, but he imagined he'd feel the same if he did. "Is that what Faith was doing when she invited you down to Tenacity? Fighting off the world?"

Amy hummed in agreement. "Letting me hide from it more like. One of their employees actually just went off on maternity leave, so it sort of worked out timing wise. Caleb and his dad needed an extra set of hands a few days a week, and here I was. But I appreciate them letting me bunk in for a while all the same."

"Guess you can't complain too much about them putting you to work then."

Amy laughed. "I really can't."

They turned onto the ranch, driving down the long stretch of gravel, the rocks nicking off the bottom of the truck. Josh parked and hopped out. Amy climbed out before he could even dare to open her door again. The look she gave him told him she knew exactly what he'd been thinking.

"So, this is it," he said, gesturing from the house he'd grown up in to the massive barn that housed his cattle.

"Why is it called Split Valley?"

"There's a creek that runs through the property," Josh said. "We'll pass it on our ride."

"Oh, that's lovely."

"It's the bane of my existence actually."

"What? Why?"

"The calves like to get themselves stuck down there."

Amy laughed. "You're telling me you have to mount calf rescue missions?"

"At least a couple times a year. Ranching is all fun and games until you're trekking through knee-deep water after some baby that's still too new to know not to run away from you."

"I'm gonna need to see that in person because it sounds hilarious."

Josh inclined his head toward the barn, the brown-gray structure towering over them. "You want to meet today's newest addition?"

"Do I want to meet a tiny, mooing ball of fluff? The answer to that is always yes."

Josh's pulse fluttered at her enthusiasm. He hurried after her as she set off for the barn door. Inside it smelled of... Well, cows and churned earth and damp straw. He led her through the building, pointing out the feed storage and various calving boxes for the expectant mothers, each of them filled with soft bedding. They walked further along a concrete aisle, coming upon a gate. He swung it open, admitting them into an area with another calving box. He'd left the mother and baby inside after the vet had come by to help with the birth and was pleased to see that both mother and baby seemed to be getting on fine. The calf was nestled down in the bedding, his ears twitching.

"Oh my God," Amy said softly. "He's so little."

"He came a bit early by the looks of things but he'll do just fine. Mama here will make sure of it." Josh kept an eye on the mother as Amy gave the calf a little pat, her face lighting up. They weren't pets. Josh knew that. But they sure were cute.

"Do you ever get used to this?" Amy said.

"Never."

"I've roped a lot of calves in the rodeo ring but they're older. This one's so precious."

"Come on," Josh said. "Let's go check out those horses before you fall in love with the little guy. My father always said you can like 'em but you can't love 'em."

"Guess not when it's your livelihood," Amy said. She reached her hand up and let Josh pull her to her feet.

She followed him out of the calving box and down into a different part of the barn. When they reached the horse stalls, they were greeted by Mac, who stuck his head over his gate for a head scratch.

Josh obliged. "This is Mac. Our resident drama queen. And that's Bella in there," he said, pointing her out in the next stall. "And Bitsy at the end."

Amy walked up to Bitsy's stall, biting her lip as she gave the horse a long look.

"Maybe you wanna take Bella out," Josh cautioned, worried as Amy opened the gate to Bitsy's stall. "Like I said... She's not the friendliest." Amy reached her hand out and Josh braced as Bitsy nosed forward. *Please don't nip at her, Bit. I'm trying to make a good impression.*

But Bitsy simply sniffed and then nuzzled Amy's hand.

Josh came up behind her, still on edge, but Amy reached her other hand up, rubbing down Bitsy's neck. "I don't know how you did that."

"You need to have some more faith in me, cowboy. I do know how to charm a horse." She ran her hand along Bitsy's back, giving her a solid pat.

"You sure you want to ride her?"

"Just get me some tack," Amy said, accepting the challenge.

Josh shook his head. This might go terribly. He left the

stall and returned with all the necessary tack. As Amy got Bitsy saddled up, Josh turned to Mac, doing the same. When they were done, he watched Amy climb into Bitsy's saddle, clicking her tongue. Bitsy headed for the door and Josh followed.

"We'll head up along the edge of the property line," he said, gesturing to a fence. Amy shifted around in her saddle. "You okay?"

"Yeah, sorry. It's just been a couple months since I've been on a horse. It always brings me a certain kind of joy when it's been this long. I get a little antsy. It's taking everything in me not to dig in my heels and gallop full-out."

"Can you try not to give me a heart attack? Bitsy's behaving for you now, but I think it's best if you ease into that sort of thing."

Amy laughed. "Worried about me?" She clicked her tongue and Bitsy trotted ahead.

Josh's stomach flipped. He liked this. He *really* liked this. He liked that he'd made her happy. He liked having her here. He liked having company on this usually lonely trail.

When Josh caught up with her, Amy was patting Bitsy on the side of the neck. "I am a little worried she's gonna try and throw you."

"She would never." Amy cooed down at her and Bitsy's ears twitched. "Though it would not be my first time falling off a horse."

"I suppose it's a hazard of the trade?"

"It doesn't happen often, but it *does* happen. I think I'm more careful now. When I was younger, I could be thrown and bounce back up like nothing had happened. Now, I'll be a walking bruise."

"Ever broken anything?"

"My collarbone," Amy said. "Once. And my wrist." She

gestured with her left hand. "Got my hand tangled in a rope and got dragged by a steer. I was back on a horse before the cast had even finished setting."

Josh's eyes widened. Amy was tougher than he thought.

"I can't imagine doing that now. So Bitsy and I are going to be good friends. Aren't we, girl?" Bitsy chuffed like she understood.

They crested the far ridge of the property and started up along the fence that kept the cattle off Juniper Road. Josh kept one eye on the fence line, forever looking for wear and tear that might need fixing. But mostly he watched the way the evening crept up on them, painting Amy in the early colors of sunset. It brought out hints of red in her dark hair and the flush in her cheeks and the blue of her eyes. For a beat he wished he could somehow preserve this moment. Him and Amy and the world around them beautifully still.

His heart raced at the thought.

"So, riddle me this," she said. "How does a man like you, with a place like this, end up out here all alone? Is it a choice or…" She let the rest of her question fade.

Josh tilted his head, wondering how to answer.

"If I've overstepped, just say so," Amy said.

"You haven't," he assured her. Past relationships weren't usually something he wanted to dwell on, but for some reason he wanted to tell Amy. Maybe just so he could explain that he was a good guy who'd simply stumbled on some bad luck as far as love was concerned. "I guess recently I'd just kind of given up on looking."

She nodded. Bitsy weaved so close he could have reached out and touched the piece of hair that had escaped Amy's ponytail.

"I… My last relationship sorta made me want to *not* try again. I thought things were going well, but Erica felt trapped here with me. So she took off for bigger and better things and… I'm still here," he said. He didn't know if he was explaining it right. "Don't get me wrong, I want to be here. This place is what makes me happiest. I just don't really need my heart stomped on again."

"I'm sorry that happened," Amy said. She glanced out across the fields. "I don't know how anyone could feel trapped here."

"I suppose the same way I'd feel totally out of my element if I was dropped in the middle of some big city."

"Still, I'm sorry you couldn't find a way forward together."

"I think in hindsight it's easier to see that maybe we weren't as great together as I always thought we were. Maybe we didn't match up in the right ways. I was content with this," he said, gesturing out at the ranch, at the gold dappled fields, at the sunset-gilded earth. "And she wanted… I don't know if *more* is the right word," he said, "because I think this is an awful lot for someone to be happy with. I guess she just wanted different things, better opportunities than what Tenacity could offer, and we didn't realize that about each other until it was too late. It was gonna hurt regardless by that point."

"I think it's easy to get caught up in who we *think* someone is. Especially when we're not really looking."

"What do you mean?"

She shrugged. "I guess it's just easy to see what we want to see. That's all."

He knew she wasn't referring to Erica rather an experience of her own. Again, he wondered about this guy who had hurt her. Wondered where he was now. What he did for a living. How he had walked away from this. From *her*.

"I like it here," Amy said.

"Yeah?"

"You were right. It's peaceful."

They fell in line beside each other again, their horses weaving together then apart.

"How does one get into rodeoing in the first place?" he asked. "I mean, I realize you're part of the Hawkins clan, but do they just line you up as kids and teach you rope tricks?"

Amy laughed. "Sort of. As a kid it just seems like fun and games and you can't wait to get on a horse. I remember spending hours watching my grandmother Hattie in the arena. She's the one who started it all, proving that anything men could do on the rodeo circuit, she could do better."

"She sounds incredible."

"Oh, she's a hoot," Amy said.

"So, how do you get from Hattie to you?" Josh asked, trying to place The Hawkins Sisters he'd always heard about with the real-life Hawkins sister sitting next to him.

"Well, Hattie's husband, Roscoe, died in a rodeo accident shortly after they were married."

"That's terrible."

"I'm sure it was," Amy said, "losing him so soon, and Hattie spent most of her childbearing years on the road, so she ended up adopting four adolescent girls. My mom, Suzie, and my aunts Josie, Hannah and Lisa. Hattie obviously taught them everything she knew, and they traveled with her on the circuit, performing and making a name for themselves as The Hawkins Sisters."

"What a legacy for Hattie to start," Josh said, impressed by the strength Hattie had clearly inspired in all her children and grandchildren.

Amy nodded in agreement. "And not just The Hawkins Sisters legacy, but even the tradition of adoption. My grandmother started that, and it's been carried on by the whole Hawkins clan. My parents adopted me and Faith, who you obviously know, but also my three other sisters, Tori, Elizabeth and Carly."

He hadn't realized she had so many sisters. "Was your dad in the rodeo, too?"

"Yeah," Amy said. "But he was forced into early retirement by a leg injury."

"Rodeoing really is in your blood."

Amy smiled. "Exactly. I spent so long surrounded by it, so long wanting to be a part of it, that by the time I realized it was something I was making a career out of, I already loved it too much to stop."

"So there was never anything else you wanted to do?"

"I don't think so. It gave me the best of everything. Time with my family." She chuckled. "Sometimes too much time. And travel. A job I loved. But in the typical sense of working some regular nine to five, I guess that was never in the cards. Working at the store is the closest I've gotten. I like being outside too much. Like being with the horses."

Josh took that in. "But there must be a bit of the glitz and glamour that you miss."

Amy shrugged. "There were definitely perks to everyone knowing your name sometimes. But the older I've gotten, the more I've realized I want other things out of life. In a way I feel like I've maybe waited too long."

"For what?"

"Oh, you know, the typical things. Marriage, kids, white picket fence. And I know I'm not that old yet, and adoption is definitely something I'd consider, it's just a feeling inside me. Like I want to settle, but I keep ending up with people that don't want me or don't want that."

I want you, he thought, almost shocking himself right out of the saddle.

"And, well, you know. It's hard some days to know you

want this thing so badly, but not know where you're supposed to look to find it. Or how long you'll have to wait for the right person to come along. Or if they ever will." She laughed. "I never used to worry about these things. I think this last relationship crashing and burning just really put things in perspective for me. Or, really, the lack of those things in my life."

Josh shook his head.

"What is it?"

"I'm still trying to figure out what kind of man let you go."

Amy scoffed. "You wouldn't believe me if I told you."

"Well, he made a mistake. A big one. One day he's gonna wake up and realize that."

She flushed the same pink as the horizon line. "I don't think so."

"I mean it."

"Thanks," she said quietly. She kept her gaze on Bitsy. "But frankly I hope I never have to see him again."

"Is he on the rodeo circuit?"

Amy hummed. "Not quite. He's sort of in that world, though. Of glitz and glamour as you said."

A world Josh would never know anything about. He wondered if Amy could ever really be okay with that. If he even stood a chance.

He hoped so.

Chapter Seven

"Morning, cowboy," Amy said as she met Josh on the street in front of the Silver Spur Café. He leaned casually against the wall of the café, hands tucked into his jean pockets, a jacket over his flannel shirt and his hair swept back beneath a Stetson. She sucked in a sharp breath. He really was the most handsome man she'd ever seen, and not for the first time she wondered what it would be like to walk down the street and hold his hand or to run her fingers along his stubbled jaw. A wave of heat washed over her, and she shoved those thoughts aside before they could gallop into dangerous territory.

"Not quite morning anymore," he said.

"You're right. Afternoon, then." Amy smiled up at him. "Should I assume we're not going to lunch since you told me to wear good shoes?"

"You assume correctly. I wanted to take you somewhere, if you're up for it?"

"Are you going to tell me where?"

He winked as he looked down at her, his eyes shadowed by the brim of his hat. "If I say no is that going to sway your decision?"

Amy hummed, narrowing her eyes. "What are you up to, cowboy?"

"Nothing, I swear." He crossed his finger over his heart. "I promise to ensure you enjoy every second of your afternoon."

"Well, in that case," she said, "lead the way."

He grinned and set off down the sidewalk, pausing long enough for Amy to fall in step beside him. Josh led them past Town Hall and the few businesses on Central Avenue before turning down an alleyway next to the Little Cowpokes Daycare Center. He cut across the parking lot behind the building, heading for a grove of trees that was fenced off. Amy slowed as they reached a gap in the fence.

"I'm starting to wonder if I agreed to this too quickly," she said as Josh slipped through the fence to stand in front of an overgrown trailhead that was blocked by a wooden gate. A no-entry sign was nailed to one of the beams.

"It'll be fine." He hopped the gate with all the grace of a mountain lion, then turned around, waiting for her.

Amy slid through the gap in the fence and stopped on the other side of the gate. "There's definitely a sign that says we shouldn't be in here."

"Do you always do what signs tell you?"

"Typically." She laughed. "I've always assumed they're there for a reason."

Josh held his hand out for her. "Then you're just gonna have to trust me. This is one sign you can ignore."

Amy bit down on her lip as butterflies exploded in her chest. She didn't want to ignore *that* sign. She wanted to trust Josh. Not just with this, but with all the feelings bubbling up inside her. She laid her hand in his, and he squeezed once before releasing her so she could scale the gate. At the top, he took her by the waist and helped her down. His fingers pressed against her sides, and her skin heated where he touched her.

"You're sure you can be away from the ranch this long?"

she asked as he stepped away. She stared into the trees, the branches parting slightly, revealing a worn trail cutting through the brush. "Aren't there afternoon chores and such?"

"There are always chores, but I've got my ranch hands covering for me." He glanced over at her as they started down the path. "I wanted to see you."

I wanted to see you.

Amy felt like she'd swallowed soap bubbles. Like the elation didn't fit in her chest. She bit down on her cheek to keep from grinning too hard. "Maybe I wanted to see you too."

"Did you?"

"Yes. But only to ask how Bitsy's doing."

Josh huffed playfully. "Of course. Now that you mention it, though, she's been all out of sorts with me since the other day. I think she misses you."

Amy nudged his arm. "I told you she was my girl now."

"Well, she used to be *my* girl. Which is why I need you to come by the ranch again sometime. Set her straight for me."

"I'll do my best, but I can't make any promises. We clearly have a bond that can't be broken."

Josh held aside a branch for her to pass. "I can't believe you've usurped my relationship with my horse."

Amy smirked. "Get used to it, cowboy. Bella and Mac are next. So, how's your day been? Other than Bitsy giving you the cold shoulder."

"No calving emergencies so far. Everyone is doing exactly what they're supposed to be doing. How's the store been? Busy?"

"Not too bad. Though we do have this one customer that keeps coming back again and again."

Josh opened his mouth to say something, but Amy plowed on.

"The weird thing is he never actually buys anything."

Josh snorted. "All right. All right. I get it."

Amy bumped his arm with hers. "To be clear, I don't mind."

"Good. I didn't plan on stopping anytime soon."

They emerged onto a wider trail, this one running along a trickling stream. Josh inclined his head, and she followed him downstream.

"You gonna tell me where we are now?" Amy asked. "Or where we're going?"

Josh gestured to an old, weather-beaten sign. "This is one of the trailheads that would have connected to the Tenacity Trail. When I was a kid, there was this big plan to revitalize it and really put the town on the map."

"And that never happened?"

He shook his head. "No. There was an incident. The money meant to fund the revitalization disappeared. And when the money disappeared, so did the folks interested in restoring the trail. Soon one small business after another folded. It was a really hard time for folks. A lot of people had to leave town, try their luck elsewhere. Most young people took off for cities with actual industry in order to find jobs."

"That's horrible," Amy said.

"Watch your step." He held his hand out, helping her over a downed tree. "Those who stayed struggled to make ends meet. I guess in a lot of ways that hasn't really changed."

"I didn't realize." They climbed down a short embankment, using the tree roots like stairs. "Tenacity has so much small-town charm."

"That's the people," Josh said. "They make all the difference and look out for each other. It isn't until you really start to look around that you see how run-down the town actually is."

Amy considered that as they came upon a pond. Streams

of sunlight broke through the canopy of leaves overhead, spotlighting growths of new wildflowers.

"Oh, Josh," she said, taken aback at how pretty and peaceful the place was. "This is…wow."

"I used to walk the overgrown trails as a boy and stumbled upon it one day. In the summer I'd hunt for crawfish along the banks." He bent down to pick up a stone from the edge of the water then skipped it across the surface. "I don't get out as much now, with all the work responsibilities, but next to the ranch, I think it's my favorite place in the world."

She could understand that. He was the kind of person who valued quiet, or at least a good place to think, and she couldn't imagine anywhere better.

"It's beautiful," she said.

"I've never brought anyone else here." He looked back at her, and Amy's heart skipped a beat. "Sometimes I'm selfishly glad that the revitalization never happened. I might have had to share this place with other people."

"Thank you for sharing it with me," she said softly. "You didn't have to."

"I wanted to."

Amy didn't know what to say to that, so she just nodded and let her hair fall in front of her face, hiding her blush. Once they'd had their fill of the burbling stream and the chilled, honeysuckle-tinted breeze, they made their way back to the trail.

She let Josh help her up the embankment. She didn't need it, but it was an excuse to hold his hand, and she took it any chance she could. At the start of the trailhead, Josh lifted her down from the gate once more, and Amy committed the thrill of it to memory. Her heart hadn't beat this hard for someone in a long time.

Maybe ever.

They passed behind the squat brick buildings along Central Avenue and cut through that alley next to the Little Cowpokes Daycare Center. People came and went from a few of the businesses, and Amy considered how difficult life must have been since the plan to revitalize the trail fell through. Still, they smiled and waved, and Josh lifted his hat. The people here were bonded by much more than by being neighbors. They were bonded by hardship.

"Do you ever wish you'd left Tenacity like a lot of the other young people?" she asked.

"It's not something I wished for necessarily. But when I was younger, I did wonder if there was another life out there I was meant to live. You know…just travel and wander and see what happens."

"As someone who did a lot of traveling and wandering, the thought of belonging somewhere, of having roots and familiarity… It's kind of nice. I really have no idea what it's like to walk down a street and look up and know the person you're passing. Or what it's like to be able to ask them about their family and their kids."

"That is nice," Josh agreed. "Being somewhere people know your history. Where friends feel more like family."

Amy nodded. Bronco was great, especially now that a lot of her family had settled there, but there was something to be said of a place where everyone would know her name and not just because she was a Hawkins sister.

Josh fit here so perfectly, and she couldn't help wishing that she'd fit here, too. Someday. When she left Bronco, she didn't think Tenacity would be somewhere she'd want to stay for long. It was supposed to be a pit stop on her road to heartbreak recovery. But now, well… Josh's hand lingered near hers, and Amy thought about how easy it would be to take it. To lace her fingers through his.

She wondered if he'd pull away. If she was being too forward. Reading too much into this.

"Back to the ranch for you?" she asked as they wandered down the sidewalk, neither of them seeming to be in a hurry.

He nodded. "Back to the store for you?"

She shrugged. "I might pop by. See how things are going. Might also just go back to Faith and Caleb's and call my mom since it's been a while. She likes her regular updates."

Josh laughed. "Mine, too. My only excuse right now is she's on a cruise with my dad. So reception isn't great."

"Oh, where are they traveling?"

"Alaska," he said. "They'd been saving for the trip for a while, and I want them to enjoy these years as much as they can. While they can. My dad's got pretty bad arthritis, which acts up a lot."

"Is that why you ended up taking over the ranch?" Amy asked.

"Partly," Josh said. "Also because, well… I was a little bit of a surprise. My mom was pretty convinced she couldn't have kids, and then I showed up when she was almost forty. My parents like to joke that I ran them ragged for those first twenty years."

"I doubt that," Amy said. "A quiet thing like you?"

Josh smirked. "You didn't know the terror I was when I was young. Anyway, by the time they were pushing sixty, they were already feeling ready for retirement. I was old enough to take on the responsibility by then, so I took over and my parents rented a small place just outside of Bronco to be closer to my dad's rheumatologist."

"Well, I hope they're having a great time."

"Me, too." He stopped walking. Amy hung back, looking at him. "There's something I've been wondering."

"What?"

"Do you think… Is there a time limit on you staying with Faith and Caleb?"

Amy raised her brow, a bit surprised by his question, wondering if he was asking for the reason she thought he was asking. "Despite what my sister might say, she loves having me here. So I don't think so."

"You got any designs on leaving?"

Her pulse raced. "Why? Would that inconvenience you?"

"Someone's gotta keep Bitsy on the straight and narrow, and she's clearly not listening to me."

"Right. The horse." Amy couldn't help the smile that stretched across her face. "Any other reason I should stick around?"

Josh took a step forward. They were close, maybe too close, and she looked up into his eyes. They were deep brown, with flecks of hazel. She could have counted each striation.

"Because I want you to?"

"Is that a question or…"

"No."

"No what?"

She could smell his soap and see the stubble along his jaw, and she lost her breath suddenly, looking at his lips.

Josh was gazing at her like he might just lean down and close the distance. But then a horn wailed, and the spell broke. Amy sucked in a sharp breath. Had he really been about to kiss her?

Josh was now glaring at a pickup truck that had stopped on the side of the road. Two men hopped out of the truck and came over to greet them.

"Amy," Josh said as they drew near, "this is Noah and Ryder Trent."

"In case it's not clear, I'm the good-looking younger brother," Ryder said, reaching for her hand.

Amy shook it.

"So, this is Amy," Noah said, also shaking her hand. He had a kind smile but looked exhausted. "We've heard a lot about you."

"Have you?" she said, glancing at Josh, who was now conveniently looking everywhere but at her.

"What're you two up to?" Noah asked, smirking like he knew exactly what they'd *almost* been up to.

Josh cleared his throat. "Took a bit of a break from work this afternoon. We just got back from walking the old trail-head."

Ryder made a face. "That's definitely a...choice."

Amy and Josh laughed in tandem. "It was nice," she said.

"You don't have to pretend for us, Amy," Ryder said. "Blink twice if you need to be rescued from this guy and his horrible attempts to show you around town."

"Really," she insisted. "It was great."

"Nah," Ryder said, looping his arm through hers. "For example, if you'd allow me to escort you this way—" he steered her down the sidewalk, gesturing with his hand "—I'd like to draw your attention to this here alleyway where our little Joshy had his first kiss."

"I didn't know this kind of tour was an option," Amy joked with Ryder. "Tell me more."

"How about we don't," Josh said.

Noah needled him in the side, making Josh flinch. "What were you, Joshy? About fourteen, I'd say. A whole group of us saw it."

Josh dropped his head into his hand and massaged his brow. "Which is why we don't need to relive it."

"I think Amy would like to hear the story," Ryder said.

"Actually, I would *love* to hear the story," Amy teased.

"I hate you both," Josh muttered to the brothers.

"He was shaking so bad I don't know how he even stood up straight," Noah said.

"I imagine you were an adorable, sweet-talking young man," Amy told Josh.

He laughed. "Oh, I was shy as anything. Couldn't get a word out. Luckily there's not a whole lot of talking needed when you're kissing."

"It went well, then?"

"Lord no." Ryder cackled. "They never spoke again after that."

"Anyway, this was my first job outside the ranch," Josh said, pointing out the barbershop.

"Stop trying to change the subject," Noah said.

"I'm not. I'm just saying, I swept up after school sometimes for extra cash."

Ryder winked. "'Cause he clearly wasn't sweeping up with the ladies, if you know what I mean."

"Okay!" Josh said, steering Ryder away. "I think she's heard enough."

Amy could just make out what they were saying from where she stood.

"Not gonna be able to call you president of Lonely Valley much longer, am I?" Ryder said.

"I think you need to go back to work."

"I'm serious, man. This is good for you. I've been saying forever that you needed to get back out there after… What was her name? Erin? Eliza?"

"Doesn't matter," Josh muttered.

Ryder looped his arm around Josh's shoulders. "That's the spirit."

Josh shrugged him off, practically escorting Ryder back to the truck. Amy would have laughed at the sight if not for the giddy butterflies dancing in her chest. Josh's friends clearly thought she was a good thing. It reassured her to know they approved of…whatever this was.

"It was good meeting you," Noah said, pulling Amy's attention. "We'll have to catch up later. We've got plenty of stories about Josh you probably want to hear."

"I'd like that," she said, then waved as the brothers drove off. She didn't miss Ryder shooting kissy faces in Josh's direction through the window.

Josh cleared his throat. "I'm really sorry about them."

"Don't be. They seem like great friends."

"For the record, you can't trust ninety percent of what Ryder says."

"Sure." Amy winked at him. "I think you just don't want me to have access to all this insider information."

"I'll tell you whatever insider information you want." Josh smiled at her so warmly she could have melted against him. "I should be getting back though."

She didn't want him to go.

"I'll call you later," he said.

Amy nodded. "I sure hope so."

Josh backed away down the sidewalk, like he wasn't quite ready to stop looking at her. Or maybe that's just what she was telling herself. When he turned around, Amy slumped down on the nearest bench, feeling like she needed to catch her breath.

Faith dumped the basket of washing on the bed between them, and Amy reached for a towel, folding it neatly and setting it aside. Next she picked up a few pillowcases, folding them into perfect little rectangles. She usually hated doing laundry, but at least with Faith as company it felt like less of a chore.

"Why do you always avoid the fitted sheets?" Faith asked as Amy tossed one sheet-looking clump back into the pile.

"Because they require an advanced degree in mathematics to fold."

Faith cocked her head and shook out the sheet. "Grab that end and help me."

Amy did, dutifully following Faith's directions as they folded the sheet.

"So, I can't help but notice that you were out with Josh. Again."

"Is there something you want to ask?" Amy said, hearing the unsaid questions in Faith's voice.

"Did you have a nice time on your walk?"

"I did," Amy said. "He took me down part of the Tenacity Trail."

Faith wrinkled her nose. "That old, overgrown thing?"

Amy laughed. "Part of the trail leads to a clearing that Josh is fond of. I guess he used to go there as a boy. It was quite beautiful."

"If you say so."

Amy hummed. It was a shame that the revitalization of the trail fell through. More people deserved to enjoy the beauty that Josh had shown her. Even so, she felt like she'd been given another small glimpse into Josh's world, and she was eager for more.

"You've been spending an awful lot of time with him," Faith said. "I wondered if maybe it's turning into more than friendship?"

Amy matched up a pair of socks before meeting Faith's eye. "I'm not sure if us talking or hanging out or whatever's happening now was ever just friendship."

"Okay!" Faith climbed onto the bed. "This is the good stuff. Keep talking."

Amy sat down, disturbing the laundry piles. "I don't know. Everything feels so easy with him. Even the silences. And he's sweet and thoughtful and my heart races when I hear that bell over the door in the store. I'm always hoping it's him. And the other day on the ranch when we went riding..." She trailed off. "Is it ridiculous to feel this way already?"

"No," Faith said. "*I* don't think so. These things sort of just happen the way they happen. Time isn't necessarily a factor. When it's with the right person, when everything clicks and makes sense, you feel like you've known them your whole life. Like there was already a hole carved out for them, just waiting to be filled."

Amy knew part of her was talking about Caleb now, and she grinned at her sister's soft expression.

"Do you think Josh feels the same?" Faith asked.

"I mean, I think there was definitely a moment today."

"A moment? What kind of moment?"

"You know."

Faith shrugged.

Amy huffed. "The kind where you lock eyes and it feels like you're just a breath away from stumbling into a kiss for the first time."

"He almost kissed you? Where?"

"On the street. When we came back from our walk. A couple of his friends showed up before we got around to it, but I was pretty sure it was going to happen."

Faith wrinkled her nose and groaned. "*Amy...* Don't let the first time be on the street where you'll obviously be interrupted."

Amy laughed. "I can't exactly curate it. The moment happens when it happens. Anyway, it caught me a little off guard, but not because I didn't want it to happen. I just didn't realize how much I wanted it to happen." In many ways, it seemed like they'd only just met, and yet Josh showed up in her life and parked himself at her side and hadn't strayed far since. Part of her felt like being with him was the most natural thing in the world. When they were apart, she missed his company: his soft, gruff words. His thoughtful questions. That dark stare. The way only one of his cheeks dimpled when he smiled. As the list went on in her head, Amy flushed. She'd wanted to kiss Josh very much. She sort of wished she could just go back to that moment. She would have closed the distance and pressed her lips to his, just to know if he felt all the same things she felt. Were there actually sparks there? Or was she just imagining everything?

"Well, you deserve to have some fun," Faith said.

"I am having fun."

"You know, I was so worried about you moping around here, I got Tori, Elizabeth and Carly on the phone."

Amy rolled her eyes. "You did not drag them into it."

"Tori told me to get you on the dating apps. She even offered to make your profile."

Amy huffed. "I can't believe you four are having secret meetings without me."

"And that's not even the group chat Elizabeth started."

"There's a group chat I'm not in?" Amy demanded.

Faith burst out laughing. "I'm just kidding. Of course not." She narrowed her eyes playfully. "Or am I?"

Amy whipped out her phone. "I'm messaging Elizabeth right now to ask."

Faith nudged her. "I really am kidding. But I've given the girls the low-down on Josh. They all agree it's a good thing. He's brought your spark back. I've missed it."

Amy wanted to deny it, but she knew Faith was right. She felt more like herself now than she had for months. She picked up a pair of her jeans, shaking them out and tugging on the waistband a bit. "I need to stop putting my clothes in your dryer," she said. "I think they're shrinking."

"There's nothing wrong with my dryer."

"It's on like turbo heat mode or something."

"If your clothes are fitting a little more snugly, maybe it's all these visits with Josh and a distinct lack of rodeo training."

That was fair, Amy supposed. She was used to a more rigorous training schedule when she was on the rodeo circuit. She'd grown complacent with her simple life since coming to Tenacity: helping out at the store and being with Josh. But it had also been such a nice change of pace, part of Amy wondered if some snug jeans were a worthwhile exchange. Maybe it could always be like this.

Maybe Josh was supposed to be something more permanent in her life.

That thought was quickly overwhelmed by another thought. Was she rushing into these feelings too quickly?

"What are you thinking?" Faith asked. "You've gone all quiet and that's never a good sign."

"I don't know. I think there's still a small part of me that feels like this is too good to be true." As wonderful as all this felt, she knew she should slow down. Hold off. Pull back.

Tru rose to the forefront of her mind. When she was away from Josh, it was easier to remember how wretched Tru had made her feel. The problem was, it wasn't like that at first. In the beginning, Tru was a total gentleman. He'd said he liked to keep his private life out of the spotlight, and Amy had been dazzled by the lengths he was willing to go to protect her from the media. He'd seemed every bit as kind and honest as his movie persona as he'd wined and dined her!

She cringed now, reliving the memory of him saying she was like no one he'd ever met. She'd fallen hard, sucked right into his trap. In all those weeks, he never once pressured her for sex, but it had gotten to the point that she was *dying* to sleep with him. He kept saying she was "worth waiting for," and Lord, had that just made her swoon harder. Around Christmas, he'd jetted her off to St. Barts, a little island paradise where they could finally be together away from the prying eyes of the media. Amy truly thought she'd found something wonderful with Tru. Only after New Year's, Tru had to fly off to Europe to film, and though he still kept in touch, as the weeks went on, communication eventually dropped off entirely. It was like a knife to the chest, and only now was Amy starting to realize the full extent of the wound Tru left behind. She'd trusted him, and not only had he basically dumped her after sleeping with her, he'd done it by marrying another woman. She was a damn fool, and that's what worried her about her own judgment when it came to Josh.

He couldn't possibly be this wonderful. Something had to be amiss.

It was true, he helped ease the sting Tru McCoy left behind. But what if he left his own wound? Amy didn't think she could handle that again. Not this soon. What if it turned out he didn't feel the same? Could she trust these feelings? Could she trust Josh?

"What if it all goes wrong?" she said.

"What if it doesn't?"

Amy flopped on her back, toppling laundry piles. "Does life really work like that?"

"I mean, it did for Elizabeth and Jake, and Tori and Bobby. Not to mention Brynn and Garret, Audrey and Jack, Corinne and Mike," she said, listing off their sisters and cousins.

"Okay, okay."

"It also seems to be working out for me and Caleb," Faith said thoughtfully. "So I'd say so. Besides, I really do think you should give Josh a chance. Don't talk yourself out of something that could be so good."

"Sometimes I worry that we're different—maybe too different?" she said, trying in vain to keep the concern from her voice. Josh lived in his small corner of the world, and Amy had ventured out to explore all of it. More than that, what she really worried about now was that she didn't exactly know who she was away from a rodeo arena. What if Josh didn't like the person she'd become? What if he wasn't interested in her if she wasn't this glamorous Hawkins Sister anymore? Though that seemed like a silly concern. He'd liked her before she told him who she was. Right?

"Your differences are probably what's drawn you together," Faith said, derailing Amy's worries. "Josh needs a little adventure in his life and maybe you want someone grounded."

"Maybe you're right."

"Gosh! Feels like I've been waiting my whole life for you to say that."

Amy snorted, but despite her concerns, one thing was clear. She was going to keep seeing Josh. Maybe he'd only end up hurting her in the end, but Amy was speeding along this barrel run, too far gone to stop it now.

Chapter Eight

"She really likes you," Josh said, failing to hide his smile as Amy rubbed Bitsy down with the stiff-bristled brush. They'd gone for a ride earlier this morning as the sun was coming up. Josh had been surprised at how eager Amy was to get out of bed early enough to watch the sunrise. When he'd picked her up this morning, greeted by a beaming smile, his heart had landed right in his stomach, kicking up butterflies. There seemed to be more and more of them swooping around his gut every time he saw her. "You didn't even have to ply her with sugar cubes to brush her."

"Of course she likes me. We've been over this." Amy ran her hand along Bitsy's silky coat. "What's not to like? I'm an excellent rider. And a fantastic conversationalist."

"Rider, yes. Conversationalist…" Josh started to tease.

"Watch yourself, Josh Aventura."

Amy looked at him over her shoulder, a few strands of her dark hair coming loose from her ponytail. Josh wanted to reach over and brush them aside. Her eyes were bright, the corner of her mouth turning up playfully. Gosh, she was pretty when she smiled. She was pretty all the time, but something about her lit up around the horses. It was like she didn't have a care in the world.

It was no wonder Bitsy liked her. Bit was a stubborn, picky

horse, and usually the last one Josh would let someone ride, but Amy had taken to her almost instantly, and Bitsy hadn't so much as huffed in displeasure.

Josh wanted to believe that Bitsy was a good judge of character, and as he looked at the chocolate-brown mare, her dark eyes clear and glassy, he wanted to believe that she was telling him that Amy was one of the *good ones*. One he should hang on to. One he could trust not to stomp on his heart.

How was it possible that the world could make so much more sense with one person around?

He'd grown more than fond of these rides with Amy. He liked wandering the outskirts of the ranch, their horses weaving back and forth as they talked about nothing and everything. He liked looking over and seeing her there, comfortable on horseback, comfortable with him. Grinning as the sun stretched across the property, shading her eyes to see the cattle way off in the distance. He liked talking to her, more than anyone else in his life, and he never worried about the stretches of silence. Already he felt assured in the quiet spent with her.

He wanted more of that. Conversation and quiet and early morning rides that left his boots dew-stained and his cheeks warm.

"Thank you for having me out again," Amy said, patting Bitsy on the forelock. She'd hung around after the ride and followed him around the ranch while he and his ranch hands completed the morning chores. She'd visited with the tiny calf again who she'd nicknamed Romeo, and had even offered to help muck out the horse stalls. Hours had passed and she still showed no sign of leaving, and frankly Josh wasn't complaining.

"Of course," he said. By now she had to know how much he enjoyed her company. They'd been together almost every day for the past couple of weeks. There was a part of him that wished she'd never leave. "You're welcome here anytime."

She glanced over at him where he leaned against the stall door. "You mean that?"

"I wouldn't have said it if I didn't mean it."

A touch of pink washed across her face. Gosh, he liked that too. He liked making her blush. Liked knowing that he wasn't the only one affected.

"I don't miss the rodeo and the training as much as I thought I would," Amy said thoughtfully, putting the brush down. She gave Bitsy one more pat then turned to him. "But the horses..." She shrugged. "That's different."

"I think Bitsy would appreciate having you out more often," he said. "To visit. To ride."

"Is she the only one?"

Josh's heart thumped in response. "I'm sure the cattle would appreciate seeing more than my ugly mug on occasion, too."

Amy laughed. "It's far from an ugly mug and I think we both know that."

"Trying to give me a compliment?"

"Probably trying and failing, cowboy," she said. She looked up as Mac stuck his head over his gate, looking for pats. "You might regret inviting me to pop by anytime."

"Oh, yeah? Why?"

Amy flashed her teeth at him. "I'm gonna teach this lot about barrel racing."

Josh snickered, the buzz transforming in his chest, and he realized his phone was ringing. "Bella might be too old for that," he said, pulling out his phone. "She's delicate now."

"Well, maybe she'll just supervise."

"Hold that thought," he said, answering the call. He stepped away. "Hey, how's it going?"

"Didn't wake you, did I?"

On the other end of the line was Shane, longtime friend and grandson of Josh's neighbors, the Coreys—Black ranchers that had lived in Tenacity for generations. Josh and Shane had grown up running around their respective family ranches together, getting in and out of trouble, jumping off hay bales, driving heavy-duty ranch equipment, and generally causing mischief. Shane's grandparents had been good friends with his own parents, and Josh was more than glad that Shane had come back to town after a stint away.

"You know I'm up with the sun."

"Didn't know if things had changed in your old age." Josh snorted.

"You got a minute to help out an old friend?"

"What's going on?"

"Part of the fence came down last night and some of the herd got out. Could use your help wrangling up cattle and getting the fence repaired. And before you hang up on me, Gram says she'll make it worth your while."

"I would have done it out of the goodness of my heart," Josh said. "But I will allow Angela to bribe me."

"Good. You got time now?"

"Yeah, just wrapping something up," he said, glancing Amy's way where she was giving Mac's muzzle a rub.

"Would *something* happen to be that girl you were telling me about?" Shane asked.

Josh could hear the grin in his voice. He didn't say anything, but Shane knew him too well.

"She's there right now, isn't she?"

"And here I was just thinking I might let you meet her."

"Bring her," Shane said. "Gram'll be ecstatic."

"You're right," Josh said, then paused thinking it through. "On second thought, Angela might be a lot."

"Can't back out on us now."

"I don't want to give you the chance to scare her away."

"Gram!" Shane bellowed on the other end of the phone, and Josh could hear him plodding across the porch. "Josh is bringing his new woman!" There was a murmured reply and Shane yelled again. "The woman he's been seeing. Yeah, the one I told you about!"

"Great," Josh muttered.

Shane snorted. "If you don't bring her now, you're gonna get an earful."

"Yeah, thanks for that." He sighed.

"Didn't you miss me, Joshy?"

"To be honest, right now I'm not really sure why I was so excited for you to come home. I'll be over soon."

"With Amy."

"To be determined." He hung up on Shane and tucked his phone into his pocket.

"Everything okay?" Amy asked, glancing up at him as he approached.

"Just the neighbors. They need a hand—some of their cattle got out."

"Oh," Amy said. "Does that happen a lot?"

"More often than you'd think. They sort of like to play follow the leader with bad ideas."

Amy chuckled.

"Do you mind if we make a little detour on the way back?" Josh asked. "If not, I'm happy to drop you off first."

"No, of course not," Amy said. "I'd like to meet your neighbors."

"Great," Josh said, glad she was up to going, and not just because it would prevent him from getting the third degree from Angela. He was mostly just glad to get to spend some more time with her. "It shouldn't take too long. *Hopefully.*"

They packed up the truck—Josh brought his tools and

some extra lumber just in case, though he suspected Otis would have everything they needed—and drove over to the Coreys'. Otis Corey, Shane's grandfather, was the salt of the earth. He'd had gray hair and wrinkles for as long as Josh could remember, and he wore it as well as he did his plaid shirts and denim overalls and cowboy boots. He was the type to put you to work while giving you advice. Josh had always had immense respect for how hard he worked and the morals he'd passed on to his own children and grandchildren. His wife, Angela, Shane's grandmother, was the tenderhearted, tough, no-nonsense counterpart. She had a warmth that instantly endeared her to you, but she wasn't afraid to set you straight, as she'd done on numerous occasions for Josh and Shane, especially when they were getting up to no good.

"So," Amy said as Josh drove down a gravel road, dust spiraling in their wake. "Give me the crash course. What should I know?"

"Okay, well," Josh started. "Shane Corey. We practically grew up together. He's been living near Helena and just returned to Tenacity after a bad breakup. His grandparents own the ranch. Otis, steady, wise, will look at you like he's staring straight through to your soul."

Amy chuckled. "Got it."

"And his wife, Angela, she's the co-owner of Little Cowpokes Daycare Center in town. She also makes the best mac and cheese in Montana—ask anyone. And if you think you've had better…" He eyed her seriously. "No you didn't."

Amy grinned back at him. "Eyes on the road, cowboy."

"I could drive these roads blindfolded."

"Please don't," she said. "There's an awful lot of cattle roaming around."

Josh turned back to the road and realized she was right. The Coreys' cattle had gathered at the edge of the road, some of them roaming back and forth. Josh slowed so there wouldn't be any accidents, and hung his head out the window, whistling and calling out to get the cattle to move out of the way. He looked at the break in the fence.

"I wonder what happened," Amy said.

"Might have come down in the last storm we had." It was the wetter part of the year still, with temperatures varying from cold enough to need gloves to warm enough to shed your coat. They'd lucked out with nice weather this past week though, and he'd spent a good portion of it outside with Amy. "Or the board was loose and an adventurous cow decided to make a break for it."

Amy turned in her seat to watch the cattle disappear as they turned onto the Coreys' property. "They sorta look like they're waiting to be picked up for a night out."

"It'd be great if they'd just realize that they could walk back the way they came."

"Now why would they make it easy for you?"

"Because I'm a nice guy." The tires crunched over more gravel. He pulled up beside an old weather-beaten truck that both he and Shane had driven up and down this road as teens. He wasn't all that sure it actually functioned anymore or if it had merely rusted in place.

"Hey," Shane called as they got out of the truck. He came clomping down the porch steps and clapped Josh on the shoulder, pulling him into a hug. His thick black hair was shorter than it had been last time Josh had seen him, which was probably Angela's doing, and he'd apparently decided to try out a neatly trimmed beard. It suited him, Josh thought, as Shane broke away, making him look older. At least until Josh spotted that too-bright smile that usually meant mischief. Then it was like they were kids all over again. But this time Josh suspected Shane was looking at him that way because Amy came walking toward them and not because he had his mind on a prank.

"Shane, this is Amy," Josh said, introducing them.

"Good to meet you," Shane said, shaking Amy's hand. "I've heard a lot about you."

"This is becoming a regular thing now," Amy said, probably referring to the fact Noah had told her the same thing.

"Don't worry. I've only been told the best," Shane assured her.

He flashed Amy a smile that usually made women swoon and Josh nudged him. He didn't need any other competition.

"So, getting tired of our poky little town yet?" Shane asked.

"Not quite," Amy said. "It's got a few interesting things going for it."

Shane threw his head back and laughed. "I hope you don't mean this guy."

"Josh said you moved back from near Helena?"

"Yeah. A breakup chased me out."

"I can sympathize there."

"A girl after my own heart. Or whatever pieces remain," Shane joked.

They walked up the porch steps and Josh introduced Amy to Angela as she popped out the door, greeting him with a hug. She was short enough for Josh to rest his chin on the top of her head for a beat. He pulled away, noting new strands of grey by her temples and new wrinkles by her eyes, but her hug had felt as sturdy as ever. That was Angela Corey in a nutshell: sturdy, fierce, with the patience of a wrangler breaking in a wild bronco. Except when it came to his love life, of course.

"You hungry?" she asked, pushing a few curling strands of hair from her face. "Look hungry to me. Come inside."

"Gram, we have to go get the cattle," Shane interrupted.

Angela waved him off. "Where're they gonna go? Not like they're gonna hitch a ride into town."

Shane rolled his eyes.

"I saw that," Angela said even with her back turned.

"I'm gonna go grab the supplies for the fence," Shane said, eyeing Josh. "Finish up here and come find me."

Angela went into the kitchen to get plates as Josh guided Amy through to the dining room.

Amy motioned over her shoulder. "Should we offer to help or…"

"No," Josh said. "Just let her do her thing."

Before Josh had a chance to say anything else, Angela returned, putting a plate of mac and cheese down in front of each of them. It was the same dishware he used to eat off of as a boy with the little daisy patterns around the edges. It was nice to see that some things never changed. He glanced at Amy as she tucked in. It was also nice to see that some things did change.

"I've heard it's the best in Montana," Amy said as Angela sat down across from them.

"You heard right," Angela said.

Josh took his first bite and waited with bated breath for Amy's reaction. Her eyes widened and suddenly she was gushing about how good it was. Josh let out a breath of relief. Not that he expected Amy *not* to like it, but Angela was serious about her cooking and Josh loved Angela like his own grandmother, and he wanted her to like Amy.

Angela gestured to the china hutch in the corner which displayed an eclectic mix of trophies and ribbons. "I've been perfecting the recipe longer than you've been alive. To award-winning results, as you can see."

"You should have opened up a restaurant instead of a daycare."

"There's still time," Angela said. She winked. "Maybe when I retire."

Josh laughed. Otis and Angela were both in their seventies and the thought of them retiring anytime soon was almost as ridiculous as someone not liking Angela's mac and cheese.

"So, you haven't been in town long?" Angela said, and Josh winced. She had her serious face on, and Angela wasn't one to beat around the bush with pretty conversation. If she wanted to know something about Amy, she'd ask her directly. Josh felt like he needed to run some sort of interference. How could he get Amy out of the house?

"No," Amy said. "I came down in February to visit my sister, Faith."

"And she's marrying the Strom boy. They're a nice couple."

Amy nodded. "I think so."

"And what do you do for work?"

"I'm on the rodeo circuit, actually."

Angela raised a brow, impressed. "What did you say your last name was?"

"Hawkins."

Angela's eyes widened.

"Angela—" Josh cut in.

"It's fine," Amy said at the same time Angela said, "Don't you have some cattle to wrangle?"

Josh knew when not to push his luck with this woman. He stood up, looking down at Amy. She gave him a little smile that he took to mean, *I'll be just fine.* And he had no doubt she would. Amy wasn't a damsel. From everything he'd seen, she was strong and independent and feisty and even that day at the store, when she'd felt sick, she'd been stubborn about letting him help her.

"Guess I'm gonna go wrangle."

"I'll help Angela with the dishes," Amy said, "then I'll come out and join you."

Josh nodded. "See you in a few."

He left the dining room, taking a detour to the bathroom to wash his hands. From there he could hear the rattle of dishes as Amy and Angela moved into the kitchen.

"So, a Hawkins Sister," Angela said. "Not much rodeoing going on in tiny little Tenacity for you."

Josh knew Angela was fishing for information.

"You're right," Amy said. "I miss the arena and my other sisters. But it's been a nice break from Bronco."

"Is it only a break?" Angela wondered.

Amy sighed. "Honestly, I'm not sure. I *think* so. Faith kind of invited me down because I was having a tough time after a breakup."

Angela hummed in understanding. "We know all about breakups around here. I mean, don't get me wrong, I'm glad my grandbaby's back. But Shane's been going through it."

"I figure I'll sit out a few rodeos and make my way back to Bronco eventually. My ex isn't exactly on the circuit, but I don't even want to chance running into him right now."

"I think getting some space is the right thing to do for most folks if you can. It helps clear your head."

"I guess that's what I was after," Amy said. "A clear head and all that."

Josh turned off the water and leaned against the bathroom sink.

"You think you found it?"

"I'm starting to." Amy said softly.

"Well, for the record, I think you two make a lovely couple," Angela said.

Josh shouldn't have been eavesdropping. His mother had taught him better. Heck, Angela would probably scold him if she knew. But he was frozen, his breath coming shallow and uneasy, like he'd just run across the pasture.

"Oh," Amy said, laughing softly. "No, it's not like that. We're just... We're friends, I suppose."

Josh's pulse skipped in his chest. Just friends? Weren't they more than that? Didn't she feel it? He certainly did. And from where he was standing, he wanted to be much more than just friends. These feelings he had for Amy... It might sound ridiculous, but they were so much stronger than they should have been after only a couple of weeks together, but sometimes when a thing was right, it settled into your bones and couldn't be altered.

That's what being with Amy felt like. She was a breath of fresh air that had spread through his lungs and revived him.

It was right, this thing between them. He knew it was; he just hadn't wanted to push her for anything, afraid that she'd bolt like a spooked horse, trampling his heart along the way. But hearing her say that they were just friends... The words boiled in his gut like an acid soup, burning and bubbling. He looked at his face in the mirror, knowing that even after this short while, losing Amy would crush him.

"You don't sound so sure of that yourself," Angela said.

"Maybe there are some feelings there," Amy admitted. "At least on my end."

The emotion inside Josh shifted so fast he almost fell back. Had she just admitted to having feelings for him? A herd of cattle could bust through the door and he wouldn't care. His entire being delighted in Amy's little confession.

"Only *some* feelings?" Angela clarified.

"No. A lot of feelings actually. More than I probably should have. Though I don't think he knows that."

"I've known Josh for a long time, and judging by the way he looks at you, there's nothing friendly about it," Angela said pointedly.

Josh should be mortified, but all he could do was smile.

Chapter Nine

A perfect Montana sunset painted the sky, the creamsicle clouds framing the pastures in pillows of crisp orange and rosy pink and sunflower yellow. It reminded Amy of cotton candy, and she almost felt like she could reach out and pluck a handful from her place on the porch.

She'd been at Split Valley for the better part of the afternoon. When Josh had invited her out riding, it had been an easy yes, but when he'd asked her to stay for dinner... Well, how could she possibly turn down a glorious spring evening like this? Josh had been quick to suggest burgers, prepared with all the fixings, and Amy wondered if he'd been working up the nerve to ask her to stay one of the other evenings they'd spent together. He'd seemed delighted when she agreed, giving her one of those dimpled smiles, and Amy knew in her gut that her feelings for him had spiraled way past friendship. She'd said as much to Faith and to Angela Corey, but this was something else. She didn't just like Josh.

What she felt... It was something more.

And the thought of him not feeling the same way almost made her want to be sick.

But then Josh looked up from the grill where he was flipping burger patties and grinned at her in a way that made her doubt such a thing was possible. Happiness welled inside her. That, and a fierce hunger. Her belly rumbled.

"Was that your stomach?" Josh laughed.

"Maybe." Amy touched her belly. "I didn't eat much for lunch, so this is a treat. I actually didn't realize how hungry I was."

"Well, glad you brought your appetite. Burgers are almost done. You want cheese and bacon on yours?"

"Is that even a question?"

"Right. We've talked about how Faith is making you suffer the turkey bacon."

"*And* whole grains," Amy added. "She should have to answer for her crimes."

"I'll put a couple extra pieces of bacon on for you then. So you can indulge."

Amy dipped her head in thanks. He was so effortlessly thoughtful. Bacon. It was such a silly thing to get emotional over, and yet she blinked back a sudden wave of tears. God, what was wrong with her? She tried not to stare at him as her cheeks flamed hotter than the grill. "I'm glad I don't have to corrupt you to my bacon-loving ways."

"No worries there. I am a red meat carnivore through and through. Poultry has its place. Just not on my burger."

"Can I do something to help?" Amy asked.

"Grab the plates? And the condiments," he said. "They're on the counter in the kitchen. Unless you'd rather eat inside. I just thought that it's shaping up to be a nice evening and we might as well keep enjoying it."

"Definitely," Amy agreed, heading for the house.

"Oh, there's potato salad too," he called.

Amy tossed a look over her shoulder, impressed.

"Don't get too excited. Angela made it."

"I'm learning so much tonight."

"I may not know my way around the kitchen that well, but I do know my way around the grill."

Amy winked. "And that's what really matters."

She slipped through the door. Walking through Josh's space didn't feel foreign the way she thought it might. It was comfortable, filled with old wooden furniture and little touches of home she figured had been left over from his mother—the checkered throw blanket tossed over the back of the couch, the cute framed cross-stitches hung along the wall, the family portraits. In the kitchen, she gathered up the essentials for dinner and took them outside, along with a glass of sweet tea for each of them.

"You were blond," she said, coming back to the porch.

"Huh?"

"As a boy. You had blond hair."

"Oh." He ran a hand through his hair, and she appreciated the way the locks parted on either side of his face. "Guess I was. It darkened up by the time I started middle school. You snooping at the family pictures?"

"Can't be snooping when they're hanging out right in the open."

Josh plated up the burgers, and they dressed them up to their liking, then sat side by side in the Adirondack chairs, watching the last of the sunset wash across the sky. It felt like such a simple thing, being there together, eating dinner, but it also felt like everything. Amy didn't know how else to describe it. How else to express the overwhelming bubble of contentment that rose up inside her. The swell of peace made her feel like she was floating. And if that was the case, she never wanted to come down.

"Good?" Josh asked, catching her eye.

"Really good," she said. "You were right. You know your way around the grill."

"I had to figure out some way to survive bachelorhood."

"Has it... Have you..." Amy wasn't quite sure how to ask what she wanted to ask. "Feel free to tell me to mind my own business," she started again.

Josh sat up in his chair. "It's okay. You can ask."

"Has it been that long since... there was someone important in your life?"

Josh opened his mouth, closed it. He sucked in a deep breath, letting it out again. "Yeah. A good long while. My previous relationship, the one with Erica, she was the last woman I was serious with. And I'm not very good at being *non-serious*, so I haven't really been dating around or seeing anyone. I'm just not so good at the going out thing and being around heaps of people all the time. I'm my best self here. On the ranch. Where I can be outside. And I appreciate that's not everyone's cup of tea."

"Well, I like *this* Josh," Amy assured him. The corner of his mouth quirked, and a coil of desire swept through her. It was getting harder to shoo these feelings away when she was with him. She wanted to run her fingers along his stubbled jawline and taste the heat of the day on his lips.

"What are you thinking?" Josh said, peering deeply into her eyes.

Amy huffed. "About how strange fate can be."

"You mean how you can stumble into the right person when you least expect it?"

"Something like that," she said.

"You feel like the right person."

Amy opened her mouth, closed it, swallowing down her gasp.

"Are you okay?" he asked.

She nodded. "Sometimes you say awfully sweet things, cowboy. And it catches me off guard."

"I didn't mean to make you uncomfortable."

"No, you didn't," Amy said. "I just—"

"What?"

"I don't know," she said honestly. There were a lot of things she wanted to say right now. But what if they ruined everything? What if Josh didn't really mean those words? Tru had used pretty words too. *You feel like the right person.* If she was wrong, this would devastate her. She caught Josh's eye, trying to untangle her thoughts. *Do you like me the way I like you, Josh Aventura?* "I guess I'm worried I'm going to say something that'll ruin this. And I've come to the realization that I don't want to lose you."

"Why would you lose me?" he asked.

"You've been really sweet to me these past weeks, Josh." His brow pinched as she said it. "But I'm not sure I like you as a friend. As only a friend, I should say. I'm not sure I ever did." The words left her in a rush, and suddenly her insides felt hollow and achy. She wanted to fill the space, fill the silence, with something. Anything. But there was nothing to do but watch the emotions shift across Josh's face. His brow furrowed, and his mouth opened, but no words came out as he struggled through confusion and then another emotion Amy couldn't confidently identify. Surprise, maybe? Was there a hint of a smile on his lips?

"So what you're saying is…"

"That I like you an awful lot," she whispered. "More than should be possible this soon." God, she wanted to bury her face in her hands, but she resisted the urge. Resisted the urge to get up and run right off the porch. Had she ever felt this way about Tru? Filled with this heart-pounding, edge-of-her-seat desire and fear and hope? She couldn't remember. Tru felt like lifetimes ago. Lifetimes that didn't matter in a world where Josh existed.

"Amy." Josh reached between them and caught her hand. "I want you to know that being here, with you, feels right in a way that I'm not sure I've ever felt."

Her breath caught. "I feel the same way."

Josh rose from his chair, crossed the short distance and leaned down, giving her plenty of time to stop him. To push him away. To tell him he'd gotten his wires crossed, but she didn't, and Josh cupped her jaw with his hand and kissed her softly.

It was only a brush of lips.

Barely even a kiss.

But it was everything.

"Was that okay?" he asked.

"Yes," she breathed.

"Good. I didn't want you to leave here tonight not knowing how I felt."

He kissed her again.

Sensation shot through her. It was electric, just that touch, and she gasped. If it all went downhill from here, then so be it. But at least she'd told him—shown him—how she felt too.

As Josh pulled away, Amy rose out of her chair. He gathered her into his arms, pulling her in for another kiss. She was reasonably tall, but he was taller, and she had to press up on her toes to deepen the kiss, tilting her head and sinking into the feel of him.

Josh's hands smoothed up and down her back. Then he turned his head slightly, breaking the kiss. Amy heaved in a breath of air as Josh pulled away enough to lean against the railing. He kept his hands on her hips, but the distance between them left room for conversation again.

"I've been dying to do that for weeks," he said, a little smile flickering across his face.

She giggled. She couldn't help it. "Why didn't you?"

"I was afraid I'd spook you."

She snorted. "Like a skittish little horse?"

"Yes. Or that I'd chase you away." He leaned down and pecked her on the corner of the mouth. "I'm still not convinced I won't."

"You won't," she assured him. She couldn't believe she was saying those words after Tru, but Josh made her want to be bold. Or reckless. Maybe both. "And, unlike Bitsy, I don't bite. You could have told me sooner."

"I didn't want to pressure you into anything." He pulled back again. "We can take this as slow as you want. I realize that you only got out of that relationship a few months ago."

Amy curled her fingers in the fabric of his shirt, tugging him closer. "That doesn't matter anymore. And I think we've been taking things slow," she said. "Considering how we both feel." Now that she knew, now that she had him like this, she didn't want there to be any more distance. She wanted to be with Josh. Here. Now. She reached up and nipped at his jaw playfully. "We don't have to stop."

Josh groaned, pressing his face against her neck. She could feel his warm breath against her skin and it was wonderful. "Are you sure?"

"*You* don't have to stop."

"Amy, I mean it. This doesn't have to happen now. It won't change how I feel."

"I think you should stop talking and kiss me already."

He did, both hands on her cheeks, and Amy felt like she was floating.

Josh deepened the kiss again, his tongue looking for entrance, and Amy let her lips fall open, let herself sink into the bliss that crept through her veins. Her heart was beating so hard, and she was breathless, and for a few moments, they let themselves be breathless. Neither of them speaking.

"God, I want you." Josh looked at her, tucking a strand of hair behind her ear. "Do you want to go inside?"

"Well, otherwise I'm gonna start stripping out here," she teased. "And I'm not sure that's a show you want your cattle to see."

Josh laughed. "They'd be scandalized for sure." He took her by the hand and led her into the house and straight upstairs to his bedroom. Amy tried to look around, tried to catalog the rustic wooden furniture and the cowboy hat hanging off the bedpost and the smell of cedar, but she was distracted as Josh's fingers trailed up beneath her shirt.

"You made your bed," she said, impressed.

"I always make my bed. Don't you?"

"Only because Faith would be grumpy if I didn't." She kissed him. "I don't see a point if I'm just gonna mess up the sheets again."

"Because that's half the fun. Give us a second to get horizontal and I'll show you just how much fun." His hands snaked up her shirt, skimming the underside of her breast. "I think this is in the way."

Amy's shirt was on the ground before she could work up words for a reply. Josh pressed against her, his hands suddenly everywhere, and she could feel the length of him. Amy tugged on his belt buckle and Josh got the message, shrugging out of his clothes while she shimmied out of hers.

They touched and caressed as they did, sending electric shivers through her body. Lord, she wanted him.

Josh reached for her again, his hands running over bare skin. "Are you on—"

"Yes," she said. "But I think we should still use a condom."

"Got it," Josh said, reaching for a drawer by the bedside. There was the crinkle of a wrapper as Amy sat down on the bed, reclining back on her elbows just so she could look at him. Every tanned, muscled inch.

He grinned at her, taking a step closer to the bed before leaning down to press a kiss to her knee. Amy fell back, eyes closed, enjoying the sensation of his lips moving from one leg to the other, slowly inching toward the place she wanted him most.

"This okay?" he said, and Amy practically arched off the bed.

"Josh, I swear if you don't touch me—"

And then he did, with his lips and his tongue, and Amy moaned. It was good, he was so good, that she practically forgot her own name as she trembled against him. He continued his way up her body, the weight of him enveloping her, and Amy kissed his lips as he settled between her hips.

"You're sure?"

"Yes," she said, and then Josh slid against her, making love to her as only a cowboy could. She arched and panted against his ear, and when she came undone, it was to the sound of her name on his lips.

Amy floated there for a long while, in the soft aftermath, content to be held.

"Did I tucker you out?" Josh asked eventually, his words a grumble as he pressed a soft kiss to her shoulder.

"I was almost asleep," she hummed. "Unless you want me to leave?"

"Don't you dare. You should message your sister though. Let her know you're staying the night so she doesn't think I kidnapped you."

"Good idea." Amy rallied enough to dig her phone out of her jeans, half hanging off the bed.

Josh's hand wrapped around her hip, holding her in place. She smiled at that.

Won't be home tonight. Don't wait up, she texted.

Faith responded immediately. Amy! Oh my God, tell me everything!

Good night, Faith, she wrote, putting her phone away before her sister could start grilling her with questions. Questions she would be happy to answer tomorrow, when she wasn't lying in Josh's bed. She rolled back over into Josh's waiting arms.

He tucked her against him, and for the first time in months, Amy felt safe and wanted. As far as a partner went, maybe for the first time in her life.

Chapter Ten

Josh woke before his alarm, the way he did most mornings, and lay in that blissful suspension between sleep and wakefulness, where he was both completely aware and fully capable of drifting off again. If not for the years of early wake-up calls to tend to the cattle and the horses, he might have been tempted by the thought of another hour. But he was used to rising with the sun, and today would be no different.

Except, it *was* different.

He stretched, suddenly aware of an unfamiliar ache in his bones. Josh was used to hard work. His muscles had long grown accustomed to the effort of labor on the ranch—trekking long distances around the property, lifting hay bales, maintaining the facilities. But this morning was different. He ached in a way that told him he'd perhaps had too much of a good thing, and then the previous night came crashing back. Dinner on the porch. Telling Amy how he felt. Kissing her. Taking her to his bed. Well then, that explained the odd exhaustion that clung to him, and Josh couldn't be happier. He grinned to himself as he sleepily reached beneath the covers for her.

Only, his hand brushed nothing but empty space, and his eyes flew open.

Josh turned his head, finding Amy's side of the bed va-

cant. He reached out again, feeling along the space she'd occupied. The sheets were rumpled but cold, and worry flared
to life inside him. He already missed her presence, and his
entire body ached with her absence. He waited for the sleep
fog to clear, but confusion settled over him like a strangling
weight and he frowned, sitting up on his elbows. With two
fingers he rubbed the sleep from his eyes.

What was going on?

When they'd fallen asleep last night, Amy had been tucked
up against him, warm and content in his arms. She'd told her
sister she was staying the night.

So what had happened between then and now?

Maybe she'd reconsidered staying with him, or regretted
their night together, and snuck away. No, she wouldn't have
set off on her own. Someone must have come to pick her up.
But wouldn't he have heard someone come down the lane?
Tires weren't exactly quiet on the gravel. None of it made
sense, and his heart sank.

Last night had been wonderful as far as he was concerned.
Holding Amy in his arms, watching as she drifted off to
sleep… He couldn't have asked for a better end to the night.
And after everything she'd said, why would she run off?

I like you an awful lot.

Her words played on repeat in his mind. He'd said that
being with her felt right and she'd agreed. So when had it all
gone wrong? Had he somehow failed to live up to her expectations? Did she finally realize that he was just some aver-
age cattle rancher? That to be with him would mean being
stuck here too?

Josh flopped down on his back, staring at the ceiling,
wishing the ground would open up and swallow him whole.
He couldn't believe this was to be his lot in life again. He
couldn't believe he'd lost Amy when he'd only just found her.

Then he heard the squeak of the pipes in the wall. Someone was running the water in the bathroom.

The bathroom! Of course. Josh almost burst out laughing. What a fool he was, panicking. There was no reason to panic. Amy had simply gotten up to use the bathroom. He pressed his hand to his face, massaging the worry lines from his forehead. He really had to let go of these fears. Amy wasn't his ex. He wanted to be able to trust her with his heart.

Then Josh heard a different sound and he sat up.

Was that retching?

He strained his ears, listening for that unpleasant sound again. Everything was quiet, and then… Yes, Amy was getting sick.

Why was she sick?

A moment later the toilet flushed and then the pipes squeaked and clattered again as the water in the sink ran. When he heard the bathroom door pop open, he looked to the hall. Amy appeared in the doorway to the bedroom, a hand pressed to her stomach, ashen-faced. She clutched the doorframe with her other hand, her fingers blanched.

Even from here he could see a slight tremble.

Immediately Josh rolled out of bed and gathered her to him. She felt clammy. Her body sagged like it was too weak to hold her up.

"I thought you'd left."

"Only made it as far as the bathroom," she said, and he could tell she was trying to make a joke.

He pushed her hair back from her face. "Are you okay?"

"I'm sorry," she muttered. "I think I have to go. I'm not… I'm not feeling well."

"Of course. I'll uh…" Where were his keys? No, first he needed pants. "I'll drive you back to Faith's."

He dressed as quickly as he could, then helped get Amy

downstairs and into the truck. There was a moment when he thought she was going to be sick again, right there on the driveway, but once she was sitting in the passenger seat, she rolled the window down and half leaned out, breathing in the fresh air.

Josh was filled with competing emotions. He was worried and anxious that something might really be wrong, and also disappointed. Last night he'd envisioned waking her up with breakfast. He wasn't a miracle worker, but he could manage eggs and bacon and coffee. Now he just wanted to get her back to Caleb and Faith's so they could figure out if she needed to see a doctor.

Was it a bug?

Or something she ate?

Oh… *Oh!*

"God, I hope it wasn't the burgers." Josh pressed on the gas, speeding down Juniper Road, spitting dust in his wake.

"No… No, I don't think so," Amy said. "If something was wrong with the meat, you'd be sick too. But you feel fine?"

He nodded. He did feel fine. Right? He took a deep breath, trying to assess if he somehow felt unsettled. Nope. He felt fit as a fiddle. "So far so good."

"See," Amy said, sucking in shallow little breaths that made him nervous.

He still wasn't convinced this wasn't somehow his fault.

"And besides," she said, "you're a great cook."

"Wasn't much cooking involved," he noted. It wasn't the potato salad, was it? Lord smite him for even suggesting such a thing. Of course it wasn't Angela's potato salad. He'd eaten it the day before. Again, if there was something wrong, he'd be just as sick.

"It wasn't your dinner. The burgers were delicious." Amy pressed her face into her hands. "God, I'm so embarrassed."

"Don't be," Josh said, still wondering if he'd inadvertently poisoned her. "Please don't be. I had a wonderful time with you. This is just—"

"Mortifying," Amy cut in.

"It doesn't change one second of the time we spent together. Don't think that." Amy leaned her head out the window again. Josh looked between her and the road, to the way her entire face pinched, a tiny crease appearing between her eyes.

"I'm sure I just caught a stomach bug somewhere." She groaned. "Oh God, I hope I didn't give it to you!" Her eyes flew open, startled as she looked at him. "Josh, I'm so sorry."

"Don't worry about me."

"How can I not worry? The first night we spend together and I infect you with some horrible stomach germ."

"You didn't infect me with anything. We don't even know what *this* is yet."

"I hope not. Cause I really do feel awful." Amy paled and reached one hand out for the dashboard to brace herself.

Josh pressed on the gas a little, trying to shake the thought that fate was laughing at him. Here he'd found this wonderful woman, and she was ridiculous enough to like him back, and now he'd given her food poisoning or something. Ryder and Noah were never going to let him hear the end of this once they found out how his latest romantic entanglement crashed and burned. He could almost hear them now... *Remember that one time the girl literally left your place throwing up? You made her sick to her stomach?*

Josh grimaced just as Amy groaned, pressing the back of her hand to her lips.

"Do you need me to..." Josh started, trying to figure out how to best help her. "Should I pull over?"

She shook her head, eyes squinted, and sat back in her seat. "No, keep going. I'm okay. I think it'll pass."

"Will it?"

"I don't know. Let's talk about something else."

"Okay, sure. What?"

"I don't know. Distract me."

"Distract you. Right." He could manage a story. "Did I ever tell you about the weekend when Shane and I almost crashed a truck into the side of Otis and Angela's barn?"

Amy snorted. "Having met Shane, I'm not even a little surprised."

"Hey, I was the voice of reason in this situation. Even at nine years old I knew it wasn't going to end well."

"You were nine?" she said, her voice rising.

"Yes. You know country kids. You learn to drive almost anything by the time you're tall enough to reach the pedals."

"So what happened?"

"Shane was a short little thing and couldn't quite reach the brakes." He shot Amy a grin as she laughed.

"You're kidding."

"I wish I was. But, you know, once we got going it was too late. I still remember us ripping through the pasture, screaming as Shane blindly tried to slam his foot down on the brake pedal. And I'm like looking over the dash, being our eyes, grabbing the wheel to dodge the cattle, and we go ripping through a hay bale and as that clears, right at the last second I spot the barn, and just yank the wheel and we careen past it, still screaming. It was the closest I'd ever come to living out an action movie."

Amy shook with laughter. Josh did too, remembering the feeling of the truck slamming to a stop as Shane finally got his foot on the brake.

"Then what?"

"I could hear Angela hollering all the way from the house. Next thing I do is look out the window, and there she is, marching straight across the pasture toward us. To this day I swear there was steam coming out her nostrils."

"What did you do?"

"The only thing I could do. I bailed out the side of the truck, ditched Shane to deal with his grandmother, and went running home. You would have thought I was a track star."

Amy laughed again. "You didn't."

"That woman put the fear of God in me. I wasn't about to let her catch me."

"And so that was it?"

"Oh no. Otis drove over to our place later, talked to my parents about what happened. Or what *almost* happened. No one was impressed. Shane and I spent many weekends after that mucking out stalls on both properties. Angela made sure we were too busy to have any more time to get up to that kind of fun."

"She put you on the straight and narrow path?"

"Oh, absolutely. Who knows how many derelict trucks I would have taken for joyrides in my youth without her intervention."

Amy shook her head and Josh was pleased to see that she didn't look quite so ashen. He pulled onto Faith's street and into the driveway, throwing the truck in Park.

"You don't have to get out," Amy started to say.

"Like hell I don't." He hopped out of the truck and met her at her door. She was already half out of the truck. "You think I'm just going to dump you on the doorstep?"

She wobbled a bit and he wrapped his arm around her, helping her to the door.

It flew open before they reached it, and Faith's smile slowly fell from her face. "Uh-oh," she said to Amy. "You look awful."

"Gee, thanks," Amy muttered.

"Don't worry," Faith said. "I'm sure it'll pass."

But before Josh could say as much as a goodbye, Amy darted into the bathroom again.

Chapter Eleven

Despite Faith's declaration, it did not, in fact, pass.

Not for a while.

Faith stood behind her, asking a thousand questions, none of which Amy was capable of answering while she was hunched over the toilet. Finally Faith got the message and excused herself, leaving Amy in relative peace for the next half hour.

Thankfully, the nausea receded, and on shaky legs, Amy went to the sink to splash some cold water on her face. What a long morning it had already been and the sun was barely up. As she looked at herself in the mirror, she could make out the dark circles that hugged her eyes. It looked like she'd pulled an all-nighter on the road between rodeo destinations instead of a night wrapped up in Josh's arms.

She took a deep breath, comforted by the thought of him, if not still a little mortified.

At least her stomach had settled.

For now.

Amy washed her hands and left the bathroom, careful with every step, somehow afraid to trigger another bout of nausea. But as she reached her room and sank down on her bed, she was feeling a little better.

"Here," Faith said, appearing in the doorway. The tie at

130 *ALL IN WITH THE MAVERICK*

the end of her braid was coming loose. She passed Amy a glass of water.

"I'm almost afraid to drink anything."

"Little sips," Faith said, the way their parents had when they were younger. "The last thing you want to do is get de-hydrated. Then it'll be off to the hospital in Bronco."

Amy grumbled. Faith was right. That's the last thing she wanted. She brought the glass of water to her lips, realizing how dry her mouth was, and took a small sip. The water went down her throat like sandpaper. She winced.

"How are you feeling now?" Faith asked.

"Exhausted. Though my stomach feels settled for the first time since this morning. Then again, maybe this is just a short reprieve. Who knows?"

"Was it something you ate?" Faith said.

"No." Amy shook her head. She repeated what she'd said to Josh. "I'm thinking it's a stomach bug, maybe." Though she was already feeling much better than she had been ten minutes ago. But just in case… "You should keep away from me. I'm already worried I gave whatever this is to Josh. I don't need you and Caleb to catch it too." Amy flopped back on her bed. "God, how can I feel so horrible and so wonder-ful at the same time?"

"Good night until this happened?" Faith asked. "You didn't respond to any of my texts."

"How could I? Josh was right there. Did you think I was going to start gushing about him while he was lying beside me?"

"You seemed really happy to ignore me."

"I was." She sighed heavily. "It was honestly the best night, Faith. Possibly the best night of my life. And I know that sounds ridiculous, but things were just different with Josh. I mean, it's new and exciting, but there's also something that feels…"

"Right?" Faith said softly.

"Yeah," Amy said. "Like I was finally where I was supposed to be, and everything just made sense."

"Good thing Josh didn't hear you say that. It'd go right to his head."

"It's not just the sex though." Amy laughed.

"I know," Faith said, sitting down next to her and patting her knee. "I get it."

Amy smiled a bit. She probably did get it. Maybe she'd felt the same way with Caleb. It was like a giddy bubble had swelled in her chest, making her light and buoyant. Like nothing could bring her down. Until this morning. "If only I didn't get sick!" Amy covered her head with the pillow. She wanted to scream. "Like, how embarrassing is that? You sleep with a guy and then throw up in his bathroom."

Faith drummed her fingers against her lips. "Amy, what if it isn't a stomach bug?"

Amy tossed the pillow aside, sitting up on her elbows so she could look at her sister. Faith was studying her, lips pursed, eyes narrowed, like she was puzzling something out. She opened her mouth, then closed it again. Amy tilted her head. "What are you talking about?"

Faith cleared her throat. "I hate to even ask this. And please don't take it the wrong way. But is it in any way possible… I mean… Do you think you could be pregnant?"

Pregnant? She huffed a laugh. Really? Pregnant? She shook her head. "No." She sat up all the way. "No, I'm not. I mean, the last time I was with anyone was back around Christmas. We were careful, thank God," she muttered. "And I took a pregnancy test weeks ago, just to be sure because things didn't work out between us, and it was negative." But by "weeks," Amy realized she meant almost three months ago. She'd taken that pregnancy test back in January. Still, it wasn't possible that she was pregnant with... *Tru's baby.* Oh, son of a—

Amy stared at Faith, wide-eyed, shaking her head in disbelief. "It can't... *I* can't."

"Oh, honey," Faith said, taking her hand. "You know those tests aren't always accurate. Or maybe you simply took it too soon or maybe it was a false negative."

"No." Amy couldn't do anything but keep shaking her head.

"Think about it. It would explain all of your odd symptoms. Maybe it would even explain this bout of sickness that doesn't seem to be a stomach bug or food poisoning."

"Morning sickness?" Amy said. "But I haven't been sick every morning."

"No, but that's not always the case for every woman. Maybe you've been really lucky so far. But there's been other signs, Amy. Think about it. Maybe one-offs, but when you add them all up together—" Faith counted things off on her fingers. "That dizzy spell you had a few weeks ago in the store, and you're always complaining about being tired. You've also been weepy, which is really out of character for you."

Amy shifted to the edge of the bed, clutching the mattress as the pieces fell into place. She'd really thought that dizzy spell was because she hadn't eaten. And of course she was tired; she spent every spare minute she wasn't at the store with Josh. And she'd always chalked the weepiness up to being dumped by Tru. But then she thought about the fact her clothes had been feeling tighter too. Her heart galloped in her chest, the beat rushing by her ears like the crash of ocean waves.

What if Faith was right and the test had been wrong?

"Have you been getting your period?" Faith asked.

Amy shrugged. "With my birth control it's virtually non-existent, so I wouldn't even know. That's why I took the test. To be sure." As reality settled over her, terror set in, and Amy's voice trembled. "God. Not now!" She covered her face with her hands. "Not when things with me and Josh are getting so good."

"Okay," Faith said diplomatically. She got to her feet, pacing in front of Amy. "Let's not panic about anything. We don't even know for sure yet. So, here's what we're gonna do. You're gonna shower so you feel more like a human, and I'm gonna run out to the drugstore to pick up a pregnancy test. Then we'll regroup, okay?"

Amy didn't say anything.

"I'm gonna go now. Try not to freak out while I'm gone."

Amy nodded. "Right. Okay." A plan. She could handle a plan. The not freaking out part... Well, she wasn't making any promises about that.

Faith left for the Tenacity Drugs & Sundries, and Amy got in the shower, scrubbing until she felt like herself again. Was that what this was? Morning sickness? *Don't think about it,* she thought as a wave of panic launched up her throat. Nothing was confirmed, and until it was, she'd be freaking out for no reason.

When she was done in the shower, she dressed and brushed her hair. By then, Faith had returned. She handed Amy a bag full of tests.

"Isn't this a little overkill?"

"Do you want to be sure or what?"

Amy took one of the tests, popped into the bathroom, and peed on the stick following all the directions. When she was done, she opened the bathroom door, and she and Faith paced, waiting for the results with bated breath.

It came back positive.

"No," Amy said. She grabbed another test and took that one. It also came back positive and the panic inside her sky-rocketed. Amy went to grab a third test but Faith stopped her. Stared at her.

"Amy," she said softly.

Amy slumped against the bathroom wall. She was pregnant. This whole time she'd been pregnant. She was going to have a *baby*. A million thoughts raced through her mind. A baby? She couldn't have a baby. She hadn't been taking care of herself properly these past months. She tried to think back to every potentially foolish decision. Had she had a drink these past four months? She'd definitely been horseback riding. And she obviously hadn't been to see a doctor. Weren't there vitamins she was supposed to be taking? Or like…things she was supposed to be planning for? Birth? Lamaze classes? She didn't know how she was supposed to be breathing!

She was sort of hyperventilating now and that clearly wasn't right. She was also thirty-five. Did that make her a high-risk pregnancy?

"What are you thinking?" Faith asked.

"A really bad word," Amy said.

Faith chuckled softly and leaned against the wall beside her. "That's fair. I probably would be too."

"I can't believe I was so stupid."

"You weren't though. You did the things you were supposed to do. Used protection. Checked. It's just one of those flukes. You know, the zero point one percent chance or whatever it is."

"Of course it would happen to me."

"I know you haven't had long to process this news, but do you know what you're going to do now?" Faith nudged her shoulder. "Whatever it is, just know I support you and Caleb and I will be here. And all of your sisters will."

Amy had no idea what she was going to do. Of course her family would be supportive. She wouldn't expect anything else. But there was so much more to this. Tru-shaped complications that she hadn't ever considered. Having his baby would mean that she would be forever tied to that man.

The corner of Faith's mouth twitched uncertainly, and she took Amy's hand, squeezing it. "Amy, you don't have to tell me if you don't want to. I did my best to stay out of the relationship when it was happening, and I don't mean to pry now, but is the baby Tru McCoy's?"

Amy nodded miserably. "The movie star and newlywed," she said with a dramatic flourish. "And I'm now apparently his baby mama."

"Wow," Faith said under her breath. "We suspected maybe you two had a thing."

"Who?"

"Oh, me, Tori, Elizabeth, Carly. We used to talk about it all the time. But I never expected this to be the result."

"Yeah. You and me both." She could only imagine how he'd respond to the news when he found out. How was she going to tell him? Did she even want to tell him? She hadn't spoken to Tru in months. He'd likely already forgotten who she was, and maybe that was for the best. Maybe there was no need to drag him back into her life.

Besides, there was something haunting her more than the thought of confessing she was pregnant to Tru and that was telling *Josh*. Where did she even begin? As she sat there, she pictured his face and tried to imagine how he would take the news. Would he feel lied to? Betrayed? Worst of all, would he look at her differently now?

Amy couldn't shake the feeling that she was about to lose him and everything they'd been building together.

It was all over, wasn't it? Horseback rides around Split Valley Ranch and lunch at the Silver Spur Café and sunsets wrapped in each other's arms.

It was all about to change.

What a mess she'd made.

Chapter Twelve

"Okay, let's talk this out logically," Faith said, clapping her hands together. She paced in front of Amy, fingers drumming against fingers as she buzzed her lips together, clearly at a loss.

"Not sure there's much logic to it," Amy muttered, staring down into her mug of now lukewarm tea.

They'd relocated to the kitchen table around midday as Faith had tried to get Amy to eat something. The only thing she could stomach at the time was toast, especially with the news swirling through her thoughts, and that made her think of Josh and the tea and toast he'd made for her the last time she was sick. At that memory, she'd immediately broken down in a bout of uncontrollable tears which had sent Faith into a panicked scramble, and she'd whipped up a loaf of chocolate walnut banana bread.

Amy had a little chuckle about it now—her tears, Faith's anxious baking. What a pair they were. She wasn't sure there was anything particularly funny about realizing you were having a baby months into the pregnancy, but she was two slices of banana bread deep now, and the chocolate seemed to have improved her mood slightly. Either that or she was finally going into shock.

"Why are you laughing?" Faith asked. She stopped pacing.

"I don't know. Sugar rush, maybe."

Faith frowned, sitting down next to Amy. "Do you want anything else? I can make… I don't know, whatever you're craving. Or I can go pick something up."

"How about you just go back to December and tell me not to sleep with Tru. Actually, go back to the Golden Buckle Rodeo and don't even let me talk to the guy."

"I wish I could. Honestly, I'd like to give the guy a good talking to after the way he treated you. Never mind the fact that you're now pregnant with his child."

The front door opened and closed and Faith fell silent.

Caleb walked into the kitchen, home from the store for lunch. He slowed, and took a good long look at them: Faith clutching Amy's hand, looking half-murderous, Amy wearing a mix of disgust and regret. Caleb picked up the sandwich Faith had left on the counter for him and took a bite, all without taking his eyes off them. "So… do I want to know?"

Faith released her hand, stood and kissed Caleb on the cheek. "I love you," she replied, "but now is not the time to ask questions."

"Okay, well, now I'm concerned."

"Just trust me. Eat your sandwich and leave in ignorant bliss."

Concern pinched his features. "Is everyone okay?" he asked. "Your sisters? Your parents?"

Faith opened her mouth to respond as Amy slumped against the table. "I'm pregnant," she cut in before Faith could answer.

"That," Faith said, looking from Caleb to Amy.

"Huh," Caleb said. He took another bite of his sandwich. The concern shifted to confusion. "*Huh?*"

"Yeah," Amy said. "That's about how I feel."

"I'm not sure what I'm supposed to say next." He clearly

meant that Amy didn't look very enthusiastic, so perhaps the default *congratulations* was the wrong choice, and he would be right.

Amy couldn't even imagine hearing that word right now. And what about when other people found out? It would be all *Oh my God, congrats, this is so exciting!* said in high-pitched voices. She'd be hugged and squealed over and she didn't even know if she wanted any of that. What she really wanted was to find the nearest horizontal surface and bury herself in blankets. She didn't want to emerge until someone figured out what to do about this mess.

"You don't have to say anything," Faith told Caleb. She ran her hand up and down his arm. "Actually, no questions or comments is probably preferable at this time." She pecked him on the cheek again.

"Understood."

He put his plate on the counter and stuffed the rest of his sandwich in his mouth. "I guess if you need anything, call me." He shot Amy a sympathetic smile before heading back to work.

"Okay, what was I saying?" Faith asked as the front door closed again. She returned to her place at the table.

Amy propped her head on her hands. "That we should be logical about this."

"Yes. Logical options."

"Which are?"

"Well, one, do you want this baby?" Faith asked simply. "I guess that's where we need to start."

Amy pressed one hand to her stomach. To the space she imagined this little life had been secretly growing inside her. If you'd asked her last week if she had any plans to become a mother in the next year, she would have said no. Not when she was still trying to sort through heartache. But now that the opportunity had presented itself... No, now that reality had busted down her door screaming, *I'm here*, things were different.

The question was no longer *if* it happened in the future. It had already happened.

"Okay, I'm having this baby," Amy said. "Where does that leave me?"

"Well, as far as I can see it, option one, you call Tru and tell him the truth. You tell him he's going to be a father and see how he takes it. And then the two of you make decisions from there about who does what and how much involvement he has in raising your child."

Amy wanted to throw up again. "I'm sure that'll go over so well with his new bride."

"Hey, that's not on you," Faith said. "That's a problem for him to sort out."

"Right. Let's hear option two."

"Option two." Faith bit her lip, perhaps considering her words. "You say nothing. You raise this baby without Tru's influence or interference."

"And what if the baby grows up and wants to know who their father is? Then I'll have to do all this in ten years anyway. And by then my child could resent me."

Faith shrugged. "Maybe you'll feel more prepared to handle Tru in ten years."

"But then I'll still have to explain to this kid why I lied. Why I kept their father a secret." Lying to her child right out of the womb didn't feel like something she wanted to do. She sighed heavily. No, she was going to have to call Tru. She was going to have to be brave and do the adult thing and tell her ex-fling that she was carrying his child. Amy's stomach flip-flopped uncomfortably.

There was a knock on the door and Faith stood to answer it.

She breezed out of the kitchen and back in so quickly Amy blinked in surprise. Faith's teeth were clenched.

"What?"

"It's Josh," Faith said. "I peeked out the curtains."

"Oh, crap! He's probably coming to check up on me." Her pulse raced more than it had at the thought of calling Tru. She wasn't ready to face Josh yet. "What do I even say to him?"

"Nothing," Faith said. "You don't have to tell him anything yet."

Amy ran her hands through her hair. He'd stopped by on his lunch break to check on her. And though the sweetness of the gesture made warmth flood through her momentarily, it was quickly replaced by cold dread. Would he hate her? Would he stop talking to her once he found out she was carrying another man's child? Tears welled in the corners of her eyes. "I don't want to lose him."

"I can tell him you're not up to seeing anyone," Faith offered. "I'll tell him you're in bed and that should buy you some more time to figure out how you want to do this."

Faith's suggestion was enticing. She wanted nothing more than to put off this conversation, but telling him she was in bed wouldn't keep Josh away.

"No," Amy said after a beat. "He'll just worry more and stop by again later." It would be better to get this over with now. Let him see that she was fine. Then he would leave and she could figure out what the hell she was going to do.

"You're sure?"

Amy nodded, though truthfully, she wasn't sure of anything. Hiding under a pile of blankets was sounding better and better by the second.

Faith left her side and a moment later returned with Josh

trailing behind her. His face relaxed the moment he saw her, and the only thing Amy wanted to do was sink into his arms and forget about everything else. At least for a little while. Faith gave her a little nod and slipped out of the kitchen, giving them some privacy.

"Hey," he said as he crossed the kitchen. She stood to meet him. "You look better than you did this morning." He reached for her, his hands gentle as he stroked a piece of hair behind her ear. "Faith said you still aren't feeling great?"

Amy tried to mask her anguish as he enveloped her. His words were too soft and his body too warm, and she couldn't hold it together. A sob broke free and her shoulders shook. God, she was losing it.

"What's happened?" he asked, holding her tighter. "Is it something bad? Amy, tell me what's going on." He pushed her away enough to see her face. Amy couldn't stop the traitorous tears from leaking down her cheeks. "Whatever it is, it'll be okay, I promise."

And then she couldn't stop herself. She hadn't intended to tell him, not before she knew what she wanted to do, but she couldn't help herself at his tenderness. The words just tumbled out. "I'm pregnant," she said, almost choking as she did. "I'm…going to have a baby."

Josh blinked down at her and she could tell he was processing. Probably thinking the words *a baby* over and over again in his mind the same way she was.

"I had no idea," she continued, feeling like she needed to explain, like she needed him to understand that she hadn't meant to string him along or trap him in any way. "The last time I… God. I used protection. I'm not walking around sleeping with every guy I meet if that's what you're thinking."

She went to turn away but he caught her by the arms. "That's not what I was thinking."

"I swear I didn't know. I would have been up-front with you if I did. I never meant to keep this sort of thing from you."

She could see the questions in the pinch of his brow. He probably had so many. So did she. But he only asked her one: "Do you love him?"

Amy hadn't been expecting that. Of all the things she expected Josh to want to know, she never expected that to be the first question he asked her. Did she love Tru McCoy? She laughed, startling them both. "No! Gosh, no. I don't. I've come to realize that our grand relationship was nothing but an illusion," she muttered. "A part he played like in one of his movies." At this, Amy clamped her hand across her mouth. She hadn't intended to out her baby's father like that. She was screwing up everything.

Josh frowned. "I don't... His movies? I'm not sure I quite get that reference."

"Maybe for the best," she said.

"Amy." Josh's tone was pleading. "Talk to me. Please."

She sighed. She'd been truthful with him so far. What was the point in lying now? She looked up at him through watery eyes. "Have you ever heard of Tru McCoy?"

Josh's jaw went slack. "Are you being serious right now? You mean Hollywood heartthrob Tru McCoy?"

"One and the same," Amy mumbled. "Though heartthrob sort of wears off when you get to know him."

"Tru McCoy is the father?" Josh said, clearly still stunned. "Wait, didn't I just read somewhere that he got married?"

Amy nodded, unable to meet his eyes. "Yes, to one of his costars. Within weeks of breaking it off with me. So that tells you how faithful he was. And how much of an idiot I am."

"Oh, Amy." Josh cursed. "That son of a—"

"I understand if this might change things between us,"

she said, cutting him off. "I get that this is a lot. It's so much to process. Maybe too much."

"I'm honestly not sure what to think right now." Josh shook his head slowly, his eyes unfocused. "But I think I should probably get back to the ranch," he said. "Chores and stuff."

"Of course." Amy bit her tongue to keep the tears from falling again. She knew it was too much for him to handle. "Yeah, you should get back."

"I'll, uh… I guess I'll talk to you later."

"Sure." She nodded as he left the kitchen. Would they talk later? Or was this goodbye? Watching him walk away now, knowing she might never see him again, was too hard, and she turned away to save herself some of the heartache.

This was just like when everything fell apart with Tru all over again.

No, Amy thought suddenly. No. Somehow, this was so much worse.

Chapter Thirteen

Josh had never been skydiving before but he felt like he'd been pitched out the side of a plane without a parachute.

He was just falling, falling, *falling*.

And he wasn't sure when he'd hit the ground.

Or how much it would hurt.

He hurried out of Faith's house without so much as a goodbye or a wave in Amy's direction. He had one singular focus, and that was to exit that kitchen before he looked Amy in the face and said completely the wrong thing.

A baby?

Amy was having a baby with a movie star. And not just any movie star. Tru McCoy. The blond, blue-eyed, ruggedly handsome cowboy of everyone's dreams. Regardless of how it had ended, at one point, he'd been the cowboy of Amy's dreams. Somehow putting a face and a name to Amy's exfling made everything worse. That was the man who had dumped her to run off and marry someone else. That was the man who had hurt her.

He was also the man that had apparently knocked her up.

Josh massaged the ache between his eyes. It thudded in the middle of his forehead. Was this the weight of his anxious thoughts? Or was his head just coincidentally going to explode? It felt like a thousand thoughts were ricocheting around his brain, and Josh had no idea what he was supposed to do now. What was the right thing to say in this situation? He tried to imagine being in Amy's position. The last thing he'd want was other people's advice, and platitudes would feel hollow. Besides, how could he sit there and promise everything would be okay when he didn't even know if that was something she wanted to hear?

Was she angry?

Scared?

Shocked?

Judging by the look on her face and the fact she'd broken down in tears, she wasn't exactly happy about this, so he was certain *congratulations* probably wouldn't go over well. But what else did you say when someone announced they were pregnant? He didn't even know where to start. Besides wanting to knock some sense into Tru McCoy, he wasn't sure he was the right man for the job.

What did he say now that the woman he lov—

Josh wrenched the door of his truck open. Leaving was for the best. He needed to screw his head on straight before it twisted off completely.

Josh climbed into his truck, backed down the driveway, and headed to the ranch, throwing himself into afternoon chores. By the time evening rolled around, he wasn't any closer to knowing what to say to Amy. He let out a heavy sigh that rattled his lips, got back into his truck, and started driving.

What he wanted most of all was to be a loving, supportive boyfriend—because that's what he was now, wasn't he? They'd been tiptoeing around this thing, around these feelings, for weeks, and Josh sort of thought that after what Amy had said last night, things between them had gotten a lot more serious. And if that was the case, and he'd read the signs clearly, then he was as good as her boyfriend. And as her boyfriend, he wanted to know how Tru could have left her like this?

Clearly he was never serious about her, likely stringing her along the way only some big-time, sleazy Hollywood actor could. And though Josh didn't know what it was like to have the father of your baby run off and marry someone else, he did know what it was to have his heart stomped on, so as torn as he was about the news, he was also sympathetic to what Amy was going through. And he was also a little ashamed of himself for just walking out on her.

Wasn't that what Tru had done?

God, he was better than this. Josh pounded his fist against the steering wheel.

He *was* better. He was just… Scared? Worried? Completely out of his depth?

He knew things were different now. They'd changed the moment the words had left Amy's mouth. He just wished he knew *how* they'd changed. Was everything that had happened between them meaningless now? Had all the moments and feelings and smiles and laughter been for nothing?

No, he reasoned. *It didn't need to be*. Tru had left Amy. He didn't want to be in her life. He'd chosen someone else. So this didn't change anything.

But as soon as he had that thought, another question rose to the forefront of his mind. What if Tru didn't want to abandon Amy once he found out she was having his child? Yes, he did just get married. And yes, he'd chosen someone else. But maybe becoming a father would force a change of heart. Maybe he'd come to his senses and see the error of his ways. He'd finally realize how wonderful Amy was and want to start this family with her.

And where did that leave Josh? Would he want to stand in Tru's way if he decided he wanted to be a real father?

Yes! Josh's heart shouted. *A thousand times yes.*

But that wasn't the right answer. He'd never want to deprive Amy and her baby of the baby's father. That was jealousy talking, and Josh knew he wasn't handling this well. He'd walked out on Amy, he was jealous of Tru McCoy, and he really wanted a drink. That might not help him in the end, but it was the only real plan he'd come up with.

His eyes drifted down the road, past the shops on Central Avenue to the sign for the Tenacity Social Club. It was a former speakeasy turned gathering place in the basement of the building that housed the town's post office and barbershop. Local musicians often performed, but Josh was most interested in the fact that he might be able to drown his sorrows there on a weeknight.

He turned into the parking lot, got out of his truck, and walked inside. It was a dimly lit space, filled with dark-stained tables. There were no televisions mounted to the ceiling here or craft brews on the menu, and Josh liked it that way.

He nodded to people he knew, which was practically everybody. Tenacity was small, but the crowd here was even smaller. The kind of place where everybody knew your name and your daddy's name and your granddaddy's. Josh didn't know if he was quite in the mood to sit down and join any of them, so he opted to take a seat at the bar instead. The bar itself was an old wooden plank with lovers' initials carved into it. It read like a who's who of Tenacity, and Josh's stomach turned thinking about Amy as his fingers brushed over the carvings.

"You look like you just got kicked by a horse," Mike Cooper said as he offered Josh a beer from behind the bar. He was a fellow rancher who often moonlighted as a bartender. He was younger than Josh, with brown curls, and a kind smile. Mike had the kind of soft, sympathetic stare that often had Tenacity locals spilling their guts, especially after a few drinks.

Josh huffed a humorless laugh. "Sorta feels that way."

"You know, this job's made me pretty good at listening." He took a couple glasses and filled them, passing them down the bar. "If you need an ear or just someone to bounce things off of, I'm not a bad option."

Josh dipped his head. He appreciated the sympathetic ear, but he wasn't about to spill Amy's business all over town. In a place like this the news would spread like wildfire and the rumors would twist and turn until it was impossible to set people straight. The last thing Josh wanted was to chase Amy out of town.

He just sipped his drink and brooded. "Not sure talking it out is gonna help much."

"That's fair," Mike said. "You can only talk around a problem so much. Sometimes you just need to take action."

If only Josh knew what that action was.

He drank his beer, and his thoughts swirled worse than before. The drink likely wasn't helping. He could go back to see Amy. Or at least call her. But after watching him walk away, would she want anything to do with him? And if he did call, what would he even say?

It was a stupid decision, but Josh told himself that another drink might help clear things up. He knew it was a lie but he could pretend for a few minutes. "I'll take another when you've got a second," he said to Mike, downing the last gulp and pushing his empty bottle back across the bar.

Mike handed him another beer on his way by with a tray of drinks destined for a table in the back. When Mike returned he started cleaning glasses.

"Do you ever think love can be hell?" Josh said.

"Figured that's what you were in here about."

"Isn't that most of your patrons?"

Mike nodded. "It's either love or land out here."

Josh almost wished it were something to do with the ranch. He could handle that. Matters of the heart were so much more complicated. Just when he thought everything was going so perfectly, just when he thought that Amy might turn out to be *the one*, the universe charged in and wrecked it all. Maybe he really wasn't suited for love. Maybe it was time he stopped looking for Mrs. Right or Ms. Right Now or Ms. Whatever.

Josh snorted. "It's definitely not the land."

"I didn't think so." Mike sighed. "I'm not a stranger to it myself, so I know that feeling."

"Been there, done that?" Josh asked.

Mike winced, his mouth pulling into a tight line. "It's really hard to find the right person, isn't it?"

"It sucks." Josh drained his beer. "Can I get another when you get a chance?"

"You can. But you're gonna trade it for your keys," Mike said, holding out his hand.

"Ah, right," Josh said. If he was going to keep drinking, then he wasn't going to be driving. He took the ring out of his pocket, slipped his key fob free and passed it across the bar. Mike dropped it in an empty glass fishbowl that sat on the counter behind him.

"You have someone you want me to call to come pick you up when you're done with this one?" he asked, uncapping another bottle and sliding it to Josh. "Or with however many drinks you need to drown out your thoughts?"

Josh's first thought was to call Amy, and he almost said as much. But that was selfish of him. He'd practically run out on her when he didn't know what to say, and now what? He was going to ask her to come and get him? To drive him home because he'd drunk a few too many instead of talking to her? How pathetic.

"You know what, I'll just call a taxi," Josh said, rethinking his plan. The service, affectionately called the Tenacity Shuttler by locals, was operated by a few ranchers who moonlighted on the side for extra cash. And though Josh knew he still shouldn't be behind the wheel, he could at least stay sober enough to call his own ride. "Do me a favor, and brew me a coffee too?"

Mike nodded. "Sure thing."

Josh took out his phone. He was confused enough about how he felt about Amy, he didn't need to leave here drunk. He opened his contacts and called the local taxi company. They picked up on the third ring. "Yeah, hi, this is Josh Aventura. I'm at the Tenacity Social Club and need a lift to 100 Juniper Road."

Mike looked up when he ended the call. "Hey, how long have you lived out on Juniper Road?"

Josh laughed and shrugged. "My whole life."

"Are there any rocks on Juniper Road?"

Josh looked at him funny. He'd just asked about rocks, right? He hadn't had that much to drink. "Plenty of them. Why?"

Mike shrugged. "It's probably nothing, but... When you were a kid, did you know Barrett Deroy?"

"Yeah, I knew *of* him." Barrett had left town about fifteen years ago with his family under a cloud of suspicion following the 'incident'. He was accused of stealing the thousands of dollars from Tenacity Town Hall meant to restore the Tenacity Trail. Town was never the same, and most people still blamed him for how rundown Tenacity had become in recent years. "Barrett was friends with Brent Woodson, who lived on one of the neighboring ranches."

Mike frowned. "Brent Woodson, as in Mayor Woodson's son?"

Josh nodded. He was very confused. Why were they talking about rocks and Barrett Deroy? As far as he remembered, when Barrett's family fled, they were persona non grata, and no one had heard hide nor hair from them since.

Mike leaned closer to him. "Does 'Look Juniper Rock' mean anything to you?"

Josh frowned. "Is that a real question or just something you do to mess with the customers?"

"Yeah, it's a real question. 'Look Juniper Rock,'" he repeated. "Is it ringing any bells?"

Josh thought about it for a minute and then said, "The Woodsons had a bunch of boulders at the edge of their property. The Stoolers live there now. Hasn't changed much in that time, but I don't remember the rocks being anything special. I couldn't imagine why anyone would want to look at them."

Mike took in his words, nodding along like everything Josh was saying was important. "Do you mind if I take a moment and call Diego Sanchez? Diego's great-uncle has been doing some private investigating for Diego's sister. She's trying to track down the Deroy family. I think this might be a clue!"

"Huh… Well, be my guest," Josh said. If Mike wanted to call Diego about some rocks, who the hell was Josh to stand in his way? Who the hell was he to anyone? He certainly wasn't Amy's husband or this baby's father. He reached into his pocket for some money and paid his tab. "I'm gonna go catch my ride."

Josh got to his feet as Mike turned away to make the call. No, he wasn't a husband or a father, but in that moment, it shocked him just how much he wished he were.

Chapter Fourteen

Amy paced the length of the kitchen, half a sandwich in one hand, and her phone in the other. She'd been staring down at Tru's contact info for the better part of an hour. It was funny. When Tru had broken things off with her to spontaneously marry his costar, she'd been devastated and heartbroken, but in the midst of all that she'd never gotten around to deleting his contact info. Now she wondered if that was fate's little way of saying they weren't quite done with each other yet. Okay, so it actually wasn't very funny at all. Amy would have much preferred never to speak to the man again.

"Do you want another sandwich?" Faith asked, standing at the counter next to Caleb. They'd been puttering around with dinner, but Faith had stopped to make Amy a sandwich when she realized she hadn't eaten anything but toast and banana bread. Amy didn't know how to tell her she wasn't all that hungry. She was full of dread and doubt, and she didn't know what to think about Josh, and with all that swirling around inside her there couldn't possibly be any room left for food.

She shook her head. "I've still got this half."

"But are you still hungry? You must be hungry. You've hardly eaten today."

"And now you're eating for two," Caleb added.

"I've been eating for two for months apparently."

Faith hummed. "I wonder if you'll have any cravings."

Amy shrugged. She wasn't much concerned with food cravings at the moment.

"You definitely have aversions. And that's a thing too, I think. Like turkey bacon. You can't stand the stuff. Must be why you always wrinkle your nose at me whenever I cook it."

Amy looked at her, deadpan. "Are you serious right now?"

Faith licked peanut butter off the end of her knife. "What?"

"Disliking your turkey bacon has nothing to do with being pregnant. Trust me." She shook her head, trying not to laugh. It felt like such a silly thing to laugh at, especially right now, when she was trying to work up the nerve to call Tru, but she couldn't help herself. "That had everything to do with you choosing a subpar bacon variety." Amy stopped laughing suddenly. "You know, Josh and I had a good laugh about that last night." She put her phone down on the kitchen table and slumped into a chair. Last night already felt like a million years ago. So much had happened since then… So much had happened to rip apart this thing she and Josh were building.

"Oh, Amy," Faith said. "He'll be back."

"I'm not sure he will," Amy said, more to herself than Faith. If this was her reality, she needed to come to terms with it. "You didn't see the way he ran out of here."

"He cares about you," Faith said. "I can see it in the way he looks at you. Trust me. You haven't seen the last of Josh."

Amy shook her head. "Even if I have, I can't really blame him, you know? I'm sure he feels blindsided and maybe even like I lied to him."

"But you didn't," Caleb said. "You had no idea about the pregnancy when you met him."

"*I* know that. And I hope he knows that. But it doesn't change the fact that we fell for each other. Maybe even imagined a future with each other. Heck, I know I was starting to.

All the while this big secret was growing between us. And now suddenly everything we thought we knew is different."

"Not everything," Faith said softly. "Not the way you feel about each other."

"I don't know," Amy said. How would Josh really feel about hanging around her while she was carrying another man's child? "It might not be something he can get past." Saying the words out loud, she hoped would make them hurt less. It was a logical argument. Something she should expect may become a reality. But it didn't make them hurt any less. They spilled over her lips like sand, rough and grainy, getting caught between her teeth and making her throat burn.

"Just give it some more time," Caleb suggested. "A man like Josh is a quiet thinker. Let him process everything that happened today. Then he'll come back around, you'll see."

Amy blinked back tears. It was useless though. They fell and she swiped her hands over her cheeks.

"Oh, Amy," Faith said. "Don't cry. Please."

"I'm not sad," she said, sniffling. "I'm angry. I'm angry that after all this time Tru McCoy is still somehow screwing me over."

"You don't need to call him right now. You can take some time to process everything, too. Josh isn't the only one who's had a world-altering bit of news dumped in his lap today."

"No. I need to call Tru because I need a plan going forward. It's been almost four months already and I can't just wing it. I'm having a baby and that baby deserves a plan. I need to know if Tru wants to be part of that plan so I can just move on with my life, I guess."

"What can I do?" Faith asked.

Amy rubbed the last of the tears from her eyes. "Get me some olives."

"Olives?"

"Yes."

Faith laughed, and Amy did too.

"Okay, we'll just run to the store before it closes." She took Caleb by the arm. "You text me and let me know if you suddenly develop a hankering for any other random foods. But we'll just cover the gamut. You know, peanut butter, pickles, salty, sweet, savory."

"Thank you," Amy said. Faith walked over and pulled Amy up into a hug.

"It's gonna be okay. You know that, right? Whatever happens. Because you've got me and Caleb and the rest of our family. And this baby is going to be so, *so* loved."

Amy nodded. "I know."

Faith kissed her cheek. "We'll be back in an hour. Try not to let Tru McCoy rattle you. He's not worth your spit," she called over her shoulder as she headed for the door.

Caleb lingered, giving her a long look. "You know, his movies aren't even that good." And with that, he followed after Faith.

Amy waited until she heard the door close and the car start in the driveway before she picked up her phone again. It was time to stop dreading this and just do it. She had to tell Tru he was going to be a father, and she had to do it today, to save her own sanity.

Oh God.

She was going to be sick again.

She pressed the back of her hand to her lips and breathed hard.

Calm down. Faith and Caleb were right. Tru McCoy wasn't anything. He was just like any other man. Hollywood heartthrob. Those words meant nothing. It had all been one grand farce in the end, probably to get her into bed. Her and however many other women he was schmoozing on the sidelines.

When the anxious wave passed, she hit Tru's contact number and lifted the phone to her ear. With each unanswered ring, her heart raced faster and faster. Maybe he was on set somewhere and away from his phone. Or he could have changed his number since they'd been together.

Then the call rang through to voicemail and she heard Tru's voice for the first time in months. It startled her, sending an unpleasant shiver up her spine. Part of her was secretly glad he didn't pick up. How awkward would that conversation have been? She would have stumbled over her words. He would have been confused hearing from her after all this time. It was better like this. She would leave him a message with all the details. That way he could get over the shock of hearing about the pregnancy first. And then they could speak about the baby when and if he called her back.

"Hi, Tru," she said as the phone beeped. "It's, uh, Amy. Hawkins," she said as an afterthought. Who knew how much of an impression she'd really left? "Sorry to bother you like this. I know it's unexpected, but…" She hesitated. She couldn't tell him about the baby like this. Not on a voicemail. "Can you give me a call when you have a chance?" she said, the words rushing out of her. "It's really important. Uh, okay thanks. Bye."

Amy pulled the phone away from her ear and winced. Well, that was somehow both better and worse than she'd expected. Nothing to do now but wait for the horrible moment he replied. Amy hadn't even had a chance to put her phone down before it started ringing. Tru's name popped up and her eyes almost bugged out of her head. He was already calling her back!

"Dammit," she muttered under her breath. She thought she'd have a little more time—maybe even a day—before he returned her call. She answered the phone, somewhat stunned. "Hello?"

"Amy, hi!" Tru said, his voice booming through the phone. Even after listening to the voicemail, it was still a shock to hear it. "It's been a minute."

"Yeah, you could say that," she said.

"How are you?"

"I mean…" Where did she even start with that question?

Tru plowed on without letting her answer. "Look, I'm really sorry about the way things ended with us."

"Tru, that's not why I'm calling," Amy hurried to say. "I—"

"I know I didn't do right by you. Trust me. I know. And I'm so glad you reached out. I wanted to, honestly. I just didn't know how to make things right. But when I saw you call, I knew this was my chance."

"Your chance for what?"

"To fix things with us," he said, like it was the most obvious answer in the world. "My romance with my costar was ill-advised."

"Your romance?" Amy practically choked on the words. "Tru, it wasn't just a romance. You *married* the woman!"

"And it was a stupid decision. One of the stupidest I've ever made."

"Tru. Look, there's something—"

"We've already filed for divorce."

Amy touched her hand to her forehead. Her thoughts were all over the place. *This* was her child's father? "I don't know what to say."

"Then don't say anything. Not over the phone. Not like this. Can I come see you?" he asked.

What the hell was she supposed to say to that? "Tru, wait," she said. Better to just spit it out and tell him the news before this went too far.

"No, I've decided. I'm coming to see you. To apologize in person. Let me make it up to you, Amy. I'll fly to Bronco," he said. "I'll come there and you'll see. You'll see how sorry I am. How much I've changed."

Amy frowned. He was talking a mile a minute. And changed? In four months? "I… I'm not in Bronco, I'm in Tenacity right now—"

"Perfect." He cut her off. "I'll come to Tenacity then. Tomorrow. I'll see you tomorrow." He hung up before Amy could say anything else.

She blinked down at the screen and contemplated calling him back, but wouldn't it be easier to have this conversation in person anyway? Before she could make up her mind, her phone rang again. It was Josh this time, and she gasped. She hadn't expected to hear from him again today after the way he rushed off.

She answered, her heart pounding. "Hi."

"Hey," he said. She could hear the murmur of voices. A lot of voices. He must be in town somewhere. A door opened and closed with a thud, and the voices died away. "I'm sorry about how abruptly I left," he said as the silence lingered.

"It's okay," Amy said. "I don't blame you for your reaction. I'm still in shock about it myself."

"Right." Some more silence. "Well, I've done some thinking, and I'm going to follow your lead here. Whatever you want to do, I will support you."

"Oh?" Amy said, a little taken aback.

"I mean it."

"Okay, that's, um… Well, it's good to hear. I actually just called Tru to try and tell him about the baby." She wrinkled her nose. She shouldn't even be telling Josh this. It would make everything worse. "He didn't really let me get a word in, but he's coming to town tomorrow. I suppose in many ways it might be easier to break the news like that instead of over the phone."

Josh got very quiet again.

"You still with me?" she asked. Maybe she shouldn't have told him Tru was coming. But she didn't want to lie to him.

"Yeah," he said, but she wasn't sure he was. Then he said, "Okay. That's...uh, good, I suppose. That'll be good. For you to tell him."

"Yeah."

"Well, um, you get some rest and call me if you need anything."

"Okay," she said. "I will. Thanks."

She hung up and stared down at the phone. Somehow this felt just as bad as him walking out.

Chapter Fifteen

Josh climbed out of the taxi at the entrance to Split Valley Ranch and gave a little wave as the car peeled off. With just three cars in their roster, the company was kept busy, even in a town the size of Tenacity. There was always someone that needed a ride or a delivery made, which left little time for chatting or meandering, which Josh preferred.

Especially right now. The last thing he needed was the driver asking him any leading questions.

One wrong slip and his business would be all over town.

Did you hear Josh Aventura got beaten out by a movie star? That guy never stood a chance. What was he thinking?

Josh grimaced at the unfamiliar voices that filled his head. He doubted anyone would really say that, at least not to his face, but he couldn't shake the dread as he lumbered down the gravel drive to the house. He'd opted to get dropped off at the road. He needed a good walk and some fresh air to clear his head, but it wasn't clearing much of anything.

Josh stuffed his hands in his pockets, feeling every bit as pathetic as he probably looked. He'd barely worked up the nerve to call Amy before he left the Social Club. Moments before the taxi showed up, he'd realized he needed to apologize for rushing out on her the way he had and for making excuses instead of processing the way he was feeling in the moment. He knew that leaving things to linger would only end up making them both feel worse.

But hearing that Tru McCoy was coming to Tenacity tomorrow was like a kick to the gut. He hadn't realized Amy would move so quickly with the news, but he supposed she couldn't really afford to wait. The baby had been a surprise, so there was probably plenty to sort out, first of which involved telling the father.

The father. He thought the words over and over, grumbling every time. Tru didn't deserve to be the father of this baby. Josh wanted to be supportive. He wanted to follow Amy's lead with this. At least, that's what he'd told himself upon walking out of the bar. He'd been so sure of himself when he dialed her number. But now the thought of Tru coming into town to sweep Amy off her feet was both devastating and nauseating in turns. It filled Josh with a wicked heat that swelled in his head and made his cheeks burn. He'd never hated someone he'd never met before. Frankly, he'd never hated anyone.

But Tru McCoy left a bad taste in his mouth.

His dad would tell him to take a step back and assess the circumstances with a clear head, reminding Josh that he was far too close to the situation if he was having thoughts like that. But that *was* the problem. He was already too close to Amy. Too close to simply step aside and pretend like none of this mattered.

He didn't want to stand aside.

He wanted to be here for Amy and the baby, but did she even want that from him? Or had everything that happened last night just gone out the window? Tru was about to ride into town like a knight on a white horse, making her promises Josh couldn't hope to match in his wildest dreams. Of course Amy was going to choose him. Why wouldn't she? Tru could offer her so much more than he could.

Tires crunched on gravel, drawing up behind him and breaking Josh from his melancholy thoughts. He perked up, turning as headlights blinded him momentarily and a vehicle pulled up close. He hadn't been expecting company, and he jumped aside.

Shane hung out the window of his truck, one hand on the wheel, creeping up slowly. "Hey, man. Everything okay?"

Josh squinted at him in the near darkness. "Hey," he said, unable to muster an ounce of enthusiasm. "Yeah."

"Saw your truck down at the Social Club. I popped inside, thought we could have a beer together, but Mike said you'd already gone home in a taxi."

"Yeah."

"You could have called me, you know?"

"Not a big deal," Josh said. Truthfully, he could have called a lot of people. He didn't though, because there was only one person he'd wanted to talk to, one person he'd wanted to be with, and anyone else would likely have asked about why he needed a ride home on a weekday. Well, maybe not Shane. He probably wouldn't even have judged Josh for it. But Josh was still getting used to having him back in town.

"So everything's just fine despite you looking as stormy as those clouds up there," Shane said. "Am I understanding things?" He cut the ignition and the truck stilled.

"About the gist of it," Josh muttered.

Shane snorted and got out of the truck. They fell in line next to each other, walking back toward the house slowly. "I can tell when you're lying, you know. I *have* known you long enough. You get all broody and avoid looking at me."

"I'm not lying," Josh said. "Relatively speaking, everything is fine. No one's hurt. No one's dying. The ranch is trucking along. You know, on a scale of one to all the cattle escaping, it's not that bad."

"Girl trouble then," Shane said with a nod.

Josh did look at him then, but only to roll his eyes.

"Don't try denying it. I could see those slumped shoulders a mile away. And I should know. I became very familiar with that look every time I clocked myself in a mirror lately." He bumped Josh's arm. "Feels just like old times, huh? When we were both in high school and couldn't get a date to save our lives."

Josh shook his head, smiling despite how wretched he felt. It did sorta feel like old times. But they were kids back then, regardless of how grown up they'd felt. Plus with their shifting infatuations from week to week, there was always someone new to get hung up on. Josh didn't want to think about anyone else. He wanted Amy, and only her. He sighed. "This feels different. Like there's more at stake."

"Because it's real now," Shane said. "Because it matters. *She* matters."

He was right. If this thing between them didn't matter, Josh would have stepped aside the moment Amy told him she was expecting. He would have wished her luck with everything and chalked these past weeks up to a good time. And maybe that's what he should still do. But something inside him refused to acknowledge that option. He couldn't walk away from her; he just didn't know where he fit anymore.

He thought it might be by her side. But was there room there with Tru?

"I'm guessing you and Amy didn't fully break it off," Shane said.

"No," Josh said immediately. "We're not… At least, I don't think so. I mean… It's complicated." He huffed a humorless laugh. How cliché. "How can you tell?"

"I figure you'd be more of a wreck if you had. I saw the way you looked at that girl when you came by the ranch. It's all Gram could talk about after you'd left. How you'd finally found a good woman who would do right by you."

Josh didn't know how to respond. Even Angela thought they were good for each other, and that meant a lot.

"So what is it?" Shane asked. "Did you find out she has a long-lost boyfriend somewhere she's still pining over? Oh, God, she isn't married, is she?"

Josh shook his head. "No, um… She's pregnant." He had no intentions of telling Mike at the bar or anyone else, but Shane was different. He used to be able to tell Shane everything. Anything. And even though Shane had been away for a while, that hadn't changed. He trusted him not to go blabbing all over town. He even trusted him to keep this from Angela. "Sorta took her by surprise. Unplanned. Unexpected. All that." At the look on Shane's face, he added, "It's not mine. She's about three or four months along I would figure."

"Wow," Shane said, the word leaving his mouth on the end of a whistle. "I was not expecting that."

"Me neither."

They walked in silence for a beat, reaching the house. Josh slumped down on the porch steps. He felt like he was carrying sandbags on his shoulders.

"And she really had no idea?"

"No. And I believe that. I don't think she would have let things get this far without telling me." She'd been adamant that she hadn't lied to him, and Josh saw no reason not to believe her.

"Must be a shock to the system. For both of you."

"Yeah."

"And the father… Is he," Shane winced, "around?"

"He's alive and well, if that's what you're wondering. I'm

not quite sure about the state of their relationship." Amy said that it wasn't good, and he'd left her, hadn't he? He'd chosen someone else. Married that girl, even. But how did you say no to Tru McCoy? If he wanted back in this baby's life…

"That's rough," Shane said.

"I'll say."

"Well, from where I'm sitting, you've got two options. One, you walk away. You let her go. She moves on. Has her baby. Plays happy house with her kid and the baby's father."

Josh didn't like that option. "And two?"

"You fight for her."

"Did you fight?" he asked, wondering about this girl that Shane had chased across Montana.

"For a while, yeah. We had our problems. Not surprise pregnancies, mind you. But we tried to make it work. *I* tried."

Josh wanted to try. He did. But the real question was, did Amy want him to fight for her? Did she want *him* when she could have Tru? The more he thought about it, the more ridiculous it sounded. Why would she ever choose him over Mr. Hollywood Heartthrob? Josh didn't think he could handle that rejection. He didn't think he could bear to fight and lose. To let Amy *and* Tru stomp all over his heart.

"You gonna be okay?" Shane asked.

Josh glanced around the darkened property. There were still a couple chores to do. So even if he wasn't okay, there were things to be getting on with. "I suppose so. I gotta check in on the cattle once more before bed."

"You want help?"

"Nah. It'll be good for me to keep busy. Get my mind off Amy and the baby."

"If you need anything," Shane said, getting to his feet, "let me know. Even if it's just a lift to the bar tomorrow to pick up your truck."

"Thanks," Josh said. "That'd be great actually. I'll call you tomorrow."

"Sounds good."

Josh watched Shane walk back down the drive to his truck. When he was gone, Josh forced himself to his feet. All he wanted to do was go inside and go to bed and hope some of this turned out to be a bad dream. But the animals needed things and they didn't care much for matters of the heart interrupting their dinner. Josh switched into his dusty, muck-covered work boots and headed out to the barn.

He called in the cattle, making sure they were fed and watered. Then he popped down to the horse stalls, mucking them out quickly before he called them in for the night.

When he was finished, he stood in the doorway of the barn and whistled. Bella and Mac trotted toward him. Bitsy stood out in the field, just a shadow against the blue-black sky, as stubborn as ever. Josh got the other two horses settled in their stalls before he returned for Bitsy, marching out across the field to get her. He brought a halter with him and strung it over her head so he could guide her back.

"Can we not do this tonight?" he said. It wasn't lost on him that Bitsy had bonded so well with Amy these past weeks. Was she missing her favorite person too?

She huffed in his face, and Josh took that as a yes.

Josh led her back to the barn as raindrops started to fall. They pattered against the roof as he got Bitsy into her stall for the evening. She immediately dunked her head in the bucket of water, taking large gulps. Josh leaned against the gate, watching her for a moment. Bitsy had really taken to Amy, but without her here, she got on with business as usual. Maybe that's what he needed to do too.

Maybe Tru coming tomorrow was for the best. It was certainly best for Amy. For her child. It didn't matter that his heart ached at the thought. He could never compete with the glamour and jet-setting. He couldn't give Amy or this baby everything they deserved.

Shane had said he could fight for Amy, but if he stood in Tru's way, all he'd be asking Amy to do would be to give up a life of certain luxury.

Josh thumped the stall door. "Night, ladies. And Mac," he said, listening to the soft braying of the horses as he left the barn, slumping through the rain to the house. He was soaked to the bone before he reached the porch, but that didn't matter. It was just another box to check off on the long list of things that had sucked today.

What really sucked was the fact that he couldn't stop envisioning everything he could have had: Amy moving into his place. Her clothes in his closet. Maybe a horse of her own in the stables.

That was probably the hardest part of today. Giving up that dream. It was foolish of him to let his mind plan for a future.

To long for it.

To want it.

Because this was what happened when he let himself want something. Charmingly handsome movie stars came bursting in to tear it all down.

Josh ran a hand through his damp hair. But why should he have to step aside? Why should he have to give up on this dream? On Amy?

He wanted her.

So, until she told him to go, shouldn't he keep trying for this future?

Then again, how could he possibly be her first choice? He'd never been anyone's first choice, and he needed to prepare himself for that reality.

Chapter Sixteen

Amy didn't know what to do with herself and had taken to dusting everything in Faith's house. Multiple times. Bookshelves and furniture and windowsills and little figurines that sat out on the coffee table.

Everything was spotless. It had already been spotless.

But that didn't stop her from swapping out her rag for a clean one and starting all over again.

She heard Faith huff from the kitchen. Amy had already been explicitly told to sit down and relax. *It's not good to stress the baby like this.*

Honestly, Amy figured her baby would understand. This was an impossible situation and the only way to keep her nerves in check was to keep her hands busy.

Tru had texted her earlier in the day to let her know that he was jumping on a flight to Billings. He texted her again when he landed and sent her a picture of the rental car he'd ordered. It was some fancy thing that had no business being in Tenacity.

Worst of all, that car would bring him right to Amy. And wasn't that a horrible thought.

Her anxiety had been multiplying all afternoon, and she could feel the uneven, uneasy trembling of her heart against her ribs. It didn't even beat, it just shook.

But why was *she* nervous? She already knew about the baby. She'd already been sitting with this news for a day, playing out what her future might look like over and over. Sometimes the murky figure by her side looked like Tru. Sometimes it looked like Josh, and her heart gave a little leap of joy. Then again, sometimes it looked like neither of them, and she'd quickly found herself accepting that as a possible reality.

So it was Tru who should be nervous. He should have paused to question why an ex was reaching out to him after all this time.

Though she doubted it even crossed his mind. If things had already soured with his wife, then Tru was probably just looking to slide back into his life pre-marriage. And that meant rekindling his former romances. Amy had come to terms with a lot these past few months, and she was under no delusions about Tru. He wasn't ever the man she thought he was. The kindness and sweetness had all been an illusion. In reality, he was an oily, slippery snake, and she had to remember that. Because while he was out there, whispering all the right words in her ear, jetting her off to private islands, there were how many other women in his contacts?

Her gaze drifted to the clock on the wall as the hour ticked down. Billings wasn't that far from Tenacity. Tru would be here anytime now. She dusted with more vigor until she heard the unfamiliar rev of an engine. Then everything inside her seized up like ice.

"Is that him making all that racket?" Faith asked, hurrying down the hall to peek out the curtains. Wisps of hair pulled free from her braid as she stealthily took in the view. "What the hell kind of car is that?"

Amy joined her at the window, watching the car recklessly race down the street. How had she ever found him impressive?

"Looks like a Porsche," Caleb said, peeking over Faith's shoulder.

"He's gonna hit one cow pie and end up spinning off into a ditch."

"And we will not be here to see it," Caleb said. "Because this is the first day off we've had together in forever and we have a date."

"We do." Faith glanced over at Amy. "Are you gonna be okay without us?"

Amy smiled a bit. "Of course. You two go have fun. This is something I have to do on my own."

"You got this," Caleb told her. "Remember. His last movie only has a thirty-three percent audience rating on Rotten Tomatoes."

She did have this. Right? Amy watched Tru get out of his car, slipping a finely made cowboy hat on his head. He dripped in finery. His leather boots gleamed and the belt buckle at his waist sparkled in the sun. It probably cost as much as that souped-up car he'd rented.

"I can't believe that's my baby's father," Amy muttered to herself. She should have known better. She'd met her fair share of men like him on the circuit, and now she felt like an idiot for not seeing him plainly. Maybe she'd just been so desperate for it to be real.

That thought touched something in her. She'd never said that out loud, but the truth was she was getting older and the little flings on the road hadn't felt right anymore. She'd wanted something stable and real. She'd wanted someone to want her the way she thought Tru had wanted her. When that fell apart, Amy didn't think she'd ever put herself out there again, and that's when Josh had stumbled into her life. She hadn't been expecting him. But he was everything that Tru wasn't—stable, real, and he wanted her. Or, at least, he had. It didn't really matter either way, because here Tru came to ruin it all over again.

Amy buzzed her lips together. "Better go get this over with." She slipped on her shoes, stepping out onto the porch.

Her hand danced over her lower belly quickly. *Here goes nothing, baby. Actually, here goes everything.*

Tru lifted his hand in greeting and flashed her a brilliant smile.

She couldn't believe she'd ever swooned over that smile. Though she'd grown quite partial to another smile lately. A closed-mouth smile with just a hint of mischief, lips curling at the edges. Eyes creased and twinkling. Every part of her wished it were Josh walking up the driveway toward her because this felt like a certain kind of nightmare. Amy never imagined seeing Tru again outside of a billboard or TV spot, and she'd certainly never envisioned him waltzing through tiny Tenacity. Her stomach flipped uncomfortably.

"Hey there, Hawkins," Tru called. He'd always called her Hawkins with affection. Or maybe she'd only thought it was affection and he was using it to keep some semblance of polite distance between them.

"Hey," Amy called, shifting from one foot to the other. She folded her arms across her chest to keep the nerves from unraveling. "You made good time."

"I didn't want to hang out in Billings too long. Once word gets out that I'm around it's gonna be nonstop pictures and autographs." He waved off the thought. "You know how it is."

"Right," she said. She did know how that was. Not to the same degree as Tru, of course. But that part of her life also felt so far away. Like it belonged to a different Amy. An Amy that hadn't started to build a life in Tenacity.

"Besides, the only person I really wanted to see was here. So I might have been a little heavy on the gas pedal."

Amy tried to smile but it didn't come out right. Tru might wish that he'd taken his time when he found out what she had to say. Her hand fell to her stomach again. Just a momentary brush. She'd been doing that a lot since yesterday, suddenly conscious of this tiny life she had growing inside her.

Tru surged up the steps toward her, and before Amy had even opened her mouth to ask him to sit down, he'd swept her up into his arms. Amy's skin crawled. It felt wrong. These arms. They didn't belong to the right person. But suddenly Tru was kissing her, and Amy's thoughts were ringing like alarms in her head.

Her eyes widened as she forced her head back. She hadn't been expecting this kind of reception.

Tru must not have noticed the look of utter shock on her face because he was too busy hugging her, whispering words into her neck. "It's so good to see you." His breath tickled her ear and she shivered. Not the good kind of shiver. The warning bells kept ringing. This wasn't going the way she'd planned. "I've missed you, Amy. So, *so* much."

She wriggled out of his arms. Delicately. Trying not to hurt him despite the way he'd treated her. She knew the kind of shock this was about to be. "Tru—"

"I know. *I know*," he said, shaking his head and dropping his hands to his hips. "What right do I have to swoop in here like this? To kiss you like this? I know what you must be thinking and what you're going to say to me now, but I beg you to hear me out." He snatched up her hands, squeezing them. Running his thumbs over her knuckles. "The marriage. It was wrong. I knew it was wrong the moment it happened. That the only person I wanted to be with was you. I knew we were making a huge mistake. *I* was making a huge mistake.

I just didn't know how to stop what I'd started. I didn't want anyone to get hurt, but I was a coward, calling that love when I knew it wasn't." He blinked at her, those big blue eyes like shimmery pools of deceit. Oh, he was good. Too bad she'd watched him do this act on the big screen. "Will you ever forgive me? Could you ever?"

"Tru, I—"

He wrapped his hands around her shoulders, pulling her close again, running his hands up and down her back. "I want us to be together, Amy. More than anything."

Amy hesitated, overwhelmed by everything. All she could think about was Josh and the way he touched her, held her. His smile. The way he laughed. The way he made her *feel*. But this was a scenario she'd never considered when she'd called Tru. A few months ago, she might have been overjoyed at Tru's declaration, but that was before Josh, before she'd really thought about who Tru was and what she deserved. Now, Josh was the only one consuming her thoughts. Still, if her baby's father wanted to make this work, shouldn't she want to try *something*? Shouldn't they want to be at least cordial for this little life they'd created? She took a step back, breaking out of his hold again. She needed space to think.

Actually, she needed a stiff drink.

But that was a no-go for the foreseeable future.

"What do you say?" Tru said. "Forgive me?" He smiled that smile that made women across the country pull their hair out screaming. The same smile that had once had her desperate for his attention. Now it didn't even set her heart racing.

"Tru," she started again. "Before you make any big decisions or big declarations, there's something you should know." He beamed at her, nodding. "I'm pregnant and it's yours. I'm sorry I didn't tell you sooner. I just found out myself."

That beaming smile dropped from his face. "You're...
What?" he said, the corner of his mouth twitching like he
expected her to shout "gotcha."

"I'm pregnant," Amy repeated, letting the words sink in.

Tru's face fell further and further. The shock ended in a
frown, his brow pinched. He looked like she'd just hit him
over the head with a skillet. Guess he wasn't as good of an
actor as he thought. He turned pale and started stammering
about dates and condoms and how could this have happened?
Then he quieted, rubbing at the scruff on his jaw. "You say
you're pregnant, but how do I really even know it's mine? I
mean, it's been months since we were together."

Amy sucked in a sharp breath. This was not the response
she was hoping for. Frankly, she didn't know what she'd been
hoping for. But it did clarify things in her mind. "I will try
not to take offense at the accusation that I might have been
sleeping around while I was with you."

"That's not what I—"

"It is what you meant," Amy said pointedly. He didn't
argue. "Anyway, I will gladly submit to a paternity test, if
this is something you want, Tru. But from the look on your
face, it's obvious that you don't want this child. And if you
don't want this child, then you don't really want me either."
She didn't think he ever did. She was just some pretty thing
to warm his bed.

"Look, Amy, I could..." Tru swallowed hard. He glanced
around, like someone might overhear them at any moment.
"...give you the money."

"Money for what?"

"To take care of it."

Wow. She'd considered the reality that Tru wanted nothing to do with this baby, but she never thought he'd ask her
to 'take care of it'.

"That won't be necessary," Amy said calmly, knowing he wasn't referring to child support.

"Listen, I—"

Amy put her hand up, interrupting him. "I will not hold you responsible for a child you want no part of," she said. "If that's what's really worrying you. I won't blow up your life and your career. But I also won't 'take care of the problem' the way you're suggesting." The moment she'd realized she was pregnant, she knew deep down that wouldn't be an option she was taking. She'd always wanted to start her own family, whether biologically or through adoption. She also had enough financial resources to care for a child. She didn't need Tru or his fame or his money. She would have this baby on her own and she would love it enough for both of them.

"Come on, Amy. Think about how much fun we could have together. I'm not ready to be a father right now."

Amy arched her brow. That much was obvious.

"Are you really ready to be a mother?"

His question didn't make her panic the way she thought it might. She knew next to nothing about having a baby or raising a child, but it didn't fill her with fear. There were definitely nerves and excitement and a little anxiousness. Was she ready? Was she prepared? No. But she *would be* ready when the time came.

"Think about it," Tru said, taking her hand and painting a picture of the life they might have. "You could travel with me." He tucked her hair behind her ear. "And I could treat you to the finest things."

Only until he found someone new. He was probably just waiting for the ink to dry on the divorce papers. Amy wanted more for herself. More for her child. And she definitely wanted better than Tru McCoy. She looked up at him and sighed. "I think it's probably time for you to go, Tru."

He nodded once, turned from her, looked back, then set off down the porch steps. He didn't even bother to argue with her and perhaps that was the most telling of all. She was never anything to him, just a good time.

He walked down the drive to his rented car and swung the door open. He looked up at her one more time. "Call me if you change your mind."

"I won't," she said. "I promise."

Tru climbed into his rental.

Amy watched him pull down the street. In a way, she supposed she owed Tru a debt of gratitude. He had given her the gift of clarity.

She pulled out her phone and called Josh. He didn't pick up.

She ended the call, wondering if she'd lost two men in one day.

One thing was certain: she was going to have this baby. Regardless of whether she had anyone by her side to help raise it.

Chapter Seventeen

Sometimes Josh hated the damn creek Split Valley Ranch was built on. Not for the first time over the years did he consider filling the entire thing in with gravel.

He closed the passenger door of his truck with a hard thud, a coil of rope slung over his shoulder. He marched across the pasture to the edge of the creek, stopping just short of where the ground dipped sharply toward the water.

He looked down at the small calf that waded through the water, tail flicking. It looked up at him, making soft snuffling sounds.

"How'd you get yourself down here, huh?"

The calf responded with a half-hearted moo before carrying on down the creek.

"Now don't go wandering," Josh called as he carefully made his way down the short embankment. It was still slick with mud from the winter thaw and his boots slipped. He caught himself, his hand sinking into muck. He huffed and carried on.

He'd spotted the calf earlier on a ride around the property. Usually a baby this small wouldn't stray far from its mother, so it must have been thirsty, and instead of using one of the water troughs, it had tumbled down the incline for a drink only to find it was a lot harder to get out again.

When Josh reached the creek bed, he winced. Water soaked through his boots and the bottoms of his pants. The creek was shallow for this time of year, barely up to his knees, but the calf darted away from him, forcing Josh to chase it.

"You're lucky you're cute," Josh muttered, surging forward and catching the calf by the scruff. It fought against him, making displeased sounds. He was a fluffy little thing, his coat a deep russet brown. When he looked up at Josh it was with two shiny black eyes. "Behave," Josh told the calf. "Or I have half a mind to leave you down here."

The calf did not behave. It butted against his thighs as he attempted to get the rope secured so he could pull the little thing out of the creek. Every time he managed to get the rope over its head, the calf would shake it off. He needed one hand to hold the animal still, but he needed both hands to get the rope in place.

"You know who'd probably be really good at this?" Josh muttered. "Amy. She'd have you roped in seven seconds flat. But I can't call her because Tru McCoy is in town, learning that he's about to be a father. So it'd be really great if you could just cooperate, okay?"

The calf mooed softly and rammed its head against Josh's thigh, clearly unimpressed with being detained. Josh wasn't that impressed either when the calf shook him off and went running down the creek.

"Don't be like that," he called. "This is for your own good." He trudged after the calf. The bottoms of his jeans were heavy and dragging.

The calf turned and mooed at him again. A little warrior's cry.

"I know, I *know*," Josh said, taking slow, careful steps so as not to startle the calf into running farther down the creek.

"But sometimes we have to do things we don't like. Which is why I'm here with you while Amy talks to her ex. Did I mention he's a movie star?"

The calf lowered his head and lapped at the water. Talking to it seemed to help. If he got used to Josh's presence, maybe he'd calm down enough to let Josh do his job.

"I obviously want what's best for her, you know? Even if what's best for her and the baby is Tru." Josh took the opportunity and lunged. He got his arm around the calf again, and this time he hung on. The calf bucked and reared back, trying to pull his head free as Josh strung the rope around him again.

"Not that I *actually* think Tru's what's best for her," he said through gritted teeth. "He sounds like a scumbag, all things considered. Like the guy knocks Amy up and immediately goes off to marry someone else. Sure, maybe he didn't know. But how are you just casually sleeping with someone while planning your nuptials with someone else? Who does that? He definitely doesn't deserve her."

The cow mooed. Maybe in agreement. Maybe because Josh pulled the rope tight. *Finally!* He stood, stretching the muscles that ached in his lower back. The calf made a few half-hearted attempts to bolt, but Josh held tight to the rope and he eventually settled.

Josh gave the little thing a pat on the head. "I'm not sure I deserve her either. Or, really, that I can provide the kind of life she deserves. Tru could give that to her though. He's got the money and the connections. And he already belongs to the world Amy is used to."

Josh staggered forward through the water, tugging on the rope. The calf resisted, tugging in the opposite direction. He was a strong little bugger.

"I can't give her those things," Josh continued. "Film premieres. And fancy dinners. And nights out in cities I've never even heard of."

Josh pulled harder on the rope.

"I… Am I supposed to just let her go?" That's not what he wanted. But he also didn't want this ache in his chest to worsen. He didn't want an Amy-sized heartbreak to get over. He didn't want his feelings to get dragged through the mud. And he certainly didn't want to be Amy's second choice— the consolation prize she settled for. If there was any part of her that wanted Tru… Well, maybe it was best, for his own sake, that Josh just stepped aside and let them figure this parenting thing out.

His arm flew forward suddenly as the calf launched into a run. Josh braced himself but it was too late. The calf took off like a shot, yanking Josh off his feet and face-first into the muddy water. He groaned, his clothes soaked through, his cowboy hat floating a few feet away.

The calf turned around and looked at him, prancing back and forth like they were playing a fun little game.

Josh grimaced, climbing to his feet. "I'm not gonna forget this."

Dripping muddy water, he snagged the rope, and climbed out of the creek, pulling the calf along. Once they crested the top of the muddy embankment, he set the calf loose. It went skipping across the pasture to join the other cattle and hopefully find its mother. Josh glared after it, wiping water from his face. He could taste mud on his tongue. What a day this was turning out to be.

Maybe it was time to consider putting up a fence to stop the cattle from getting stuck down there. He marched back to his truck. All he wanted to do was head to the house and take a long, hot shower. Maybe call Shane and see if he felt like a beer so he could take his mind off Tru McCoy.

His phone was blinking with notifications when he settled in the driver's seat. He picked it up, realized it was a missed call from Amy, and his heart skipped a beat.

There was no voicemail, so he called her back immediately.

"Hey," he said when she answered.

"Hi, cowboy." She sounded tired.

"Sorry I missed your call. I was…" Getting bested by a calf a third of my size? "Dealing with a little cattle situation on the ranch."

"That's okay, I know you're busy."

Not too busy to talk to you, he wanted to say, but he didn't know if that was the kind of thing she wanted to hear right now. "How'd everything go with Tru?"

"About as good as I expected, honestly."

Josh held his breath. What did that mean?

"Tru's gone," she clarified. "And I'm pretty sure he won't be back."

"So he didn't—"

"Want anything to do with the baby? No."

The rest of his breath left him in a rush. "I'm sorry, Amy."

"It's probably for the best. I'm not sure he'd make a great father right now. Or ever."

He was apologizing and part of him meant it. Amy deserved someone who was going to take responsibility for the child. Tru should have been that person. He had all the means to be that person. And the fact that he'd already failed Amy more than once made Josh angry. But there was a larger part of Josh that was quite relieved to hear this. Elated, even. If Tru was out of the picture, did that mean he and Amy could go back to the way things were? That they could just pick up where they'd left off?

But could he really compete with the memory of a movie

star? Could he get over being the person she settled for? Mostly he wondered if she could really be happy living a quiet life in Tenacity when she was used to a life of adventure. Josh worried that he knew the answer to that question and it filled him with defeat. "I really am sorry things didn't work out with Tru," he said.

"I'm not," Amy said quietly.

Silence lapsed between them, and Josh didn't know how to fill it. What the hell was he doing? He wanted Amy. But she couldn't possibly want him in the same way, especially not now that she was expecting a baby. She needed support and structure and so many other things he didn't even know about.

"Well," she said. "I'll let you get back to cattle stuff."

"Right. Yeah... I better do that."

"I guess..." Her words lingered for a long moment. "I'll talk to you later?"

"Yeah," Josh said awkwardly. He had no idea when later might be, and he felt horrible about that as the call ended. This didn't feel like a goodbye, but he also wasn't quite sure what they were anymore. Here he was ragging on Tru for not stepping up, but Josh didn't know the first thing about having a family of his own, so how could he possibly be any better than Tru McCoy?

Chapter Eighteen

"You want to stop for food?" Faith asked as they turned onto the narrow stretch of highway leaving town.

"There's not really anything worthwhile between here and Bronco," Amy said. "Just that little shack of a diner with the stale coffee."

"And the oatmeal cookies that taste like cardboard. Yeah, I know. I meant when we get into Bronco. Might be nice to have some options for a change. Don't get me wrong. I love Tenacity, I really do. But—"

"They don't have your favorite chickpea falafel wrap?"

Faith glanced at her, a smile on her face. She reached over and squeezed Amy's hand. "It's gonna be a good day. Everything's going to turn out fine at the doctor's. So I think we can make time for a little fun, too. Maybe we can even swing by the arena if you're feeling up for it. Visit with the horses. Catch up on all the rodeo gossip."

It felt like eons since Amy had been in the Bronco Convention Center or set foot in the arena. She brushed her hand across her belly. It might be a good long while before she had another chance. "Well how can I say no to that?"

Amy had never fully appreciated Faith's ability to soothe nerves. She'd been up all night thinking about this OB appointment, tossing and turning as anxiety-inducing questions ricocheted around her brain. They were on their way to see Dr. Rangely, an obstetrician who worked out of Bronco. Amy had also grown quite fond of Tenacity, but her options for medical care were more limited there than they were in the city. Plus she'd wanted to be seen as soon as possible and Dr. Rangely had an opening in her schedule.

Now that Amy knew about the baby, she was certain she'd done something wrong. Many things, probably. Her thoughts turned protective. She just wanted everything to be okay. This poor baby had already been rejected by its father. Somehow Amy had to do and be enough for this child.

"Hey," Faith said, breaking her from her anxious spiral. "Really. Everything's going to be fine."

"I just feel like the baby's not even here yet and I'm already screwing this up somehow," Amy said.

"You haven't screwed up anything. I bet you that if you talk to any new parent they feel the exact same way."

"I didn't even bother to notice I was pregnant for four months, Faith. All the signs were there."

Faith shrugged. "You had other things on your mind." Her eyebrows wiggled. "Josh-shaped things."

Amy frowned.

"How's that going by the way?"

"It's not," she said, a little defeated. "We honestly haven't spoken much since the day Tru left. I thought it might reassure him, knowing that Tru wasn't going to be around to get in the middle of what we had going on. He seemed happy about that part at least. But he has sort of retreated since then." Almost a week had passed since their phone call, and though Josh texted her on occasion, things felt different. There was a distance there she didn't know how to fix. "I think it kind of dawned on him that I was still gonna have this baby. And that being around me, being *with* me, automatically included that now."

"Amy, I don't think Josh is—"

"Of course he is. He's probably wondering if he could raise another man's baby. Wouldn't that be what you were thinking?"

Faith grew quiet. Contemplative.

"I don't think there's anything I can do but give him space," Amy said. She wasn't going to beg him to want her. The same way she hadn't begged Tru to want this baby. It would hurt if Josh ultimately stepped away, but she would survive it. She *had* to survive it. There was someone more important than herself to think about now.

"I think you need to have more faith in Josh."

Amy smirked a bit. "That's your advice? Have faith."

"Hey, if anyone's qualified to give that advice, it's me."

"I think I'd rather just be practical, and not live with some fairy-tale hope right now."

They passed a sign for Bronco. Amy glanced at her phone. They'd made good time, but they wouldn't be able to squeeze in lunch before the appointment. That was fine though. Amy was too nervous to eat. Just as she was thinking it, her stomach made a noise to the contrary.

"Well," Faith said. "You be practical and I'll hold out enough hope for both of us. Josh is a good man."

"I'm not disputing he's a good man. But I also once foolishly thought Tru was a good man."

Faith snorted. "You were clearly off your rocker with that one. Even I could have told you to tread lightly there. And I was a big Tru McCoy fan until recent events."

"I fell for the oldest trick in the book. Listening to anything that sweet-talking snake had to say." Amy's pulse skipped as Faith pulled into a parking lot outside a squat red-bricked building with Bronco Medical on the side in fancy silver letters. "I just don't want to do that again."

Faith parked and turned to face her. "Okay, listen here. Josh Aventura is nothing like Tru. Yes, he's a gruff, stubborn man. And maybe it's gonna take him a minute to realize the good thing he's got here, but he *will* realize it, Amy. Just don't give up on him yet."

Amy flashed her a tight, close-lipped smile. She wanted to believe Faith more than anything, but the best thing to do was have reasonable expectations. It would soften the blow when it landed. "I haven't given up. Not completely." She glanced out the window and back. "I just have other things on my mind."

"Speaking of other things. Let's go see how this little avocado is doing."

Amy chuckled. "Avocado?"

"Oh, yeah, I was reading on this app that the baby is the size of an avocado now or something."

"Explains why all my pants are tight."

They got out of the car and walked into the building. Amy was greeted by a receptionist who took her name and checked her in. Then they sat down in the faux-leather chairs that filled the waiting room. Amy glanced around at the other patients, wondering how many of them had been unexpectedly knocked up by famous movie stars. Maybe there was a club for that sort of thing.

"We should get a pony."

"Hmm?" Amy glanced over at Faith.

"For the baby. It's gonna have to learn to ride sometime."

Amy tilted her head, briefly resting it on Faith's shoulder. "Let's just focus on getting to the due date before we start teaching it rope tricks."

"I am so excited."

Amy was lucky. What did she need Tru for when she had Faith?

"Amy?" a nurse called, waving her back. She was short, with a full head of gray hair and wore her glasses on a chain around her neck.

Amy liked her immediately. She hopped up.

Faith caught her hand and squeezed. "I'll be here when you get out."

The nurse led her to an exam room and had Amy change into a gown. She took some vitals and some blood and chatted with her, completing a basic history. Then she asked Amy to pee in a cup. When the doctor came in, she shook Amy's hand.

She was a tall, middle-aged woman with dark, curly hair.

"Doctor Rangely," she said. "But you can call me Gloria."

"Amy. Nice to meet you."

"So, babies," the doctor said, grabbing a seat in a swivel chair.

"Babies," Amy repeated.

"Your first?"

"Yes."

"And are we happy about that?" There was no judgment in her voice, and Amy suspected the doctor asked most of her patients this question. Their answer likely determined the direction of the conversation.

"It was definitely unexpected, and I'm not going to say I wasn't shocked, but yes… I'm happy."

"Okay, then. I'd like to do an ultrasound. Just to see where we're starting off since this is your first visit with me."

"We're gonna see the baby?"

Dr. Rangely nodded. "You bet." Amy reclined back on a table, her heart pounding, as the doctor rubbed cold jelly on her stomach. She tried to imagine what this would have been like if Tru had decided to play parent. Would he be standing here next to her, holding her hand? She couldn't picture it, but she could picture Josh and her chest ached. Dr. Rangely adjusted some equipment, pulling a monitor into focus as she moved the ultrasound wand over Amy's skin. Amy watched the screen, trying to make sense of the unrecognizable blurs.

Suddenly a swooshing sound filled the room.

"Is that—"

"The heartbeat," Dr. Rangely said.

"The heartbeat," Amy replied softly. The swoosh raced faster than Amy expected. "Is that…good?"

"That's normal. It's a very strong heartbeat."

Amy wanted to burst into tears. And she did. "I'm sorry," she muttered as she was handed a box of tissues. Everything was just so uncertain. She didn't know where she stood with Josh or how to fix this situation or if there was any chance she might get him back, but the baby's heart was strong. How could everything be so wrong and so right at the same time? "I guess I just wanted to make sure everything was okay. After not knowing for so long, and not doing the things I was supposed to do—"

"Everything looks really good, Amy," Dr. Rangely said. "I promise. Nothing out of the ordinary for this far along."

"I was reading some things on the internet and it said you weren't supposed to be horseback riding. But then some other websites said you could. And I did. Go horseback riding, that is. But that's before I knew about the baby."

Dr. Rangely rubbed the back of Amy's hand where it rested on her stomach. "It can be a risky activity, especially for people who aren't used to it. But your file said you worked the rodeo circuit, right?" Amy nodded. "Well, seeing as you do it regularly, I'd say you were probably okay."

Amy let out a sigh of relief.

The doctor removed her gloves. "You and the baby look healthy. But I'd like you to hold off on the horseback riding going forward. You're into the second trimester now, and you're technically high-risk because of your age. You're fit but we want to be as careful as we can."

"I can do that," Amy said.

Dr. Rangely sat down at a desk, making notes on a laptop. "We'll get you scheduled for the anatomy scan next. We'll be able to tell you the sex at that appointment if you want to know."

"When's that?"

"Between eighteen and twenty-two weeks."

Amy felt her breath leave her. At the next scan she'd learn if she was having a little boy or a little girl. This was all becoming more real by the second, and she couldn't help wishing for Josh. Wishing that he'd been here with her, listening to this baby's heartbeat, the baby they might raise together if any part of him still wanted her. But could he ever want her enough now to make that work? Emotion filled her chest and it was hard to breathe.

Dr. Rangely turned to her. "Now, do you have any questions for me?"

"Oh, so many," Amy said. "Is it true the baby is the size of an avocado?"

"A baby!" Elizabeth said as they crowded into a booth. "I can't believe it. Congratulations again. I'm going to keep saying that. I'm so happy for you. I know you've wanted this for a while."

"A secret baby!" Tori added, nudging Carly. "This is like one of those episodes of *I Didn't Know I Was Pregnant*. I keep trying to get Bobby to watch it with me, but he just thinks it's ridiculous."

"Oh my God, you're so right!"

"I always wondered about those stories," Faith said, sipping her sweet tea. She'd gathered up all their sisters at Lulu's BBQ for lunch, surprising Amy after the doctor's appointment, and Amy's heart was full to bursting. And not just because she was starving, and Lulu's ribs were her favorite of anywhere in Bronco. "Like how do you reach nine months and not know you've grown a whole child?"

"Well, I *do* know I'm pregnant now," Amy said. "And according to Dr. Rangely, the baby is officially the size of an avocado."

There were squeals of delight around the table, and Amy had to hush her sisters so as not to disturb the other customers with their excitement. It had been an emotional morning, hearing the heartbeat and missing Josh, but despite everything, Amy was looking forward to welcoming this baby into her life, and knowing that her sisters supported her was the biggest gift of all.

"Your little avocado," Elizabeth said on a sigh. "I remember those days. Enjoy these moments. Pregnancy will go faster than you think. I'm not saying it's all sunshine and rainbows—"

"Yes, the morning sickness made sure of that," Amy said.

The corner of Elizabeth's mouth turned up. "I don't miss that, but there are definitely other moments you'll miss. Feeling the baby kick for the first time, watching your bump grow."

Amy smiled softly, considering her words. Elizabeth had lost her first husband, but she'd remarried Jake McCreery, and between them they now had five kids. If any one of her sisters should be offering parenting advice, it was definitely Elizabeth. "Well, I can't say I'm looking forward to giving up horseback riding for the foreseeable future—" she laid her hand on her stomach "—but I suppose some sacrifices are worth it."

"I guess that's you off the rodeo circuit for a while longer," Tori said. "At least for the duration of the pregnancy and some maternity leave."

"Yeah." Amy sighed. "I wasn't in any big rush to get back to it, honestly. At least, not until this nonsense with—"

"Yes!" Carly interrupted. "Let's talk about Tru. How is the baby daddy doing?"

Tori hushed her, looking around like their conversation might attract the paparazzi.

Amy's eyes cut across to Faith, who threw her hands up. "Like I was going to be able to keep that a secret."

"It's not like we didn't know," Elizabeth said diplomatically. "Or we at least suspected you two had something going on. When we learned you were pregnant and how far along you were, it wasn't hard to put two and two together."

Amy grumbled. "I was a fool. I know, I *know*."

"You were in love," Tori said, patting her hand. "There's a difference."

"What I can't understand is why a man with Tru's money and resources can't be bothered caring for his child," Carly said. "It's not like you're expecting him to tote the baby down a red carpet in a stroller. But he could at least kick over a bit for formula. Or set the kid up with a small trust fund for school or whatever."

"Caleb says he's too full of himself to genuinely care about anyone else in his life," Faith said.

Amy nodded. "I can't help thinking that maybe his rejection was a blessing in disguise. I mean, Tru's not cut out to be any kind of parent. That became more than obvious when I last saw him. And throwing this baby into the limelight, for the tabloids to exploit before the baby can even understand the situation, feels cruel. If there's one thing I want to be able to do as a mother, it's protect this child. Even if that means protecting them from their own—"

"Father?" Carly cut in.

Amy hesitated. "He's not, though, is he?" She'd been thinking more and more about this since the ultrasound this morning. Lying there on the exam table, alone, she'd come to the conclusion that Tru was *not* this baby's father, not in the sense that he should be. "He might have donated his DNA, but he's never going to do all the things a father is supposed to do."

Her sisters nodded, and Amy knew they understood. Maybe better than most. Being adopted really gave them a different perspective on what family was. It had nothing to do with DNA or blood. All that mattered were the people who stuck around in the end.

The people who chose you.

"Tru didn't choose me or this baby. So, I don't plan to tell him when the baby is born. He won't be at the hospital with me. I don't even plan to write his name down on the birth certificate." She would tell her child, one day, when they were ready to hear the truth, but until then, she didn't see a reason to weigh them down with the disaster that was Truett McCoy.

"Is there someone else's name you want to write down?" Elizabeth asked quietly, eyeing her over a plate of corn bread.

Amy opened her mouth, closed it, emotion clogging her throat. It was so hot and tight she couldn't get the words out. Tears gathered at the corners of her eyes. When she thought about that moment, about bringing this little life into the world, the only person she saw by her side was Josh.

"Oh, honey, I didn't mean to make you upset." Elizabeth reached across the table and squeezed her hand.

"It's not you," Amy said. "Honest. I'm just… I'm missing Josh. I feel like we were moving in a really good direction and now it sort of feels like I've been bucked off the back of a horse. I don't really know where we stand or where to go from here."

"Well, that's easy enough to figure out," Tori said.

Amy looked up at her.

"You know exactly what to do when you get bucked off."

"Get up, dust yourself off and get back on the horse," her sisters chorused, making Amy chuckle.

"Advice from the great Hattie herself," Tori said, raising her glass of sweet tea.

"I'm not sure that applies here," Amy said.

"Of course it does," Tori said. "Has Josh explicitly said he doesn't want to be with you?"

"Well, no," Amy said. "Not in so many words."

"Not in any words," Faith cut in.

"Has he stopped answering your texts?" Carly asked.

"No. He hasn't really called much in the last week, but he's messaged to check in. I've been trying to give him as much space as I can."

"And did you ever think that maybe he's trying to do the same thing?" Elizabeth suggested.

Carly nudged her under the table. "It sounds like he's still interested, Amy."

"I agree," Tori said. "And as far as I'm concerned, you have to get back on the horse."

Try again, Amy heard in Hattie's voice. *Don't let fear stop you from reaching for something you love.* Frankly, she knew Hattie had been talking about reaching for the reins, but maybe her sisters were right. She shouldn't give up on her and Josh yet.

She just didn't know how to reach for him. It felt unfair

to dump this kind of news on Josh and expect a decision so quickly. If she was going to ask him to choose her and this baby, she felt like she needed to give him the appropriate amount of time to process. But how long was that? Weeks? A month?

Maybe she'd just put it off forever. That would be easier than getting rejected.

"I think you're scared," Elizabeth said, squeezing her hand again. "And that's understandable."

"What if he doesn't choose me?" Amy blinked heavily. "I don't know if I can do this."

"That's what loving someone is," Elizabeth said. "It's giving them the ability to hurt you but trusting them not to. I know it's terrifying, but I really think you need to put your faith in Josh now. You need to give him a chance."

"Regardless of what happens," Tori said. "You'll always have your family. We'll be here for you and this baby."

"Trust me, Amy," Elizabeth said. "If he's the right man for you, it'll work out. But it can't work if you don't fight for it."

Chapter Nineteen

The morning had started off reasonably cool, but after a couple hours of standing under that Montana sun, lugging lumber back and forth, Josh was sweating. He took a swig from his water bottle, kneading his back. In an effort to take his mind off Amy, he'd decided to tackle the bridge repair on the eastern end of the property. It was the bridge the cattle used to cross the creek to reach the furthest pasture, and after the winter they'd had, Josh had noticed a couple of the boards rotting.

But once he'd pried up the first few, he figured he might as well just change them all, only that had turned into a bigger job than he'd anticipated. Now he was not only drenched in sweat, but his mind had started wandering, inevitably landing on Amy. All he wanted to do was call her, but something scared him off. He couldn't shake the thought that he wasn't good enough for her. And if she was only settling for him, then he'd always play second fiddle to Tru McCoy. Maybe these were ridiculous thoughts, but it's what rattled through his brain with every strike of his hammer against wood.

Josh collected another board from his truck and carried it across the bridge. He carefully dropped it in place, then secured it with half a dozen nails. He was just hammering in the last one when he spotted a cloud of dust coming up the drive.

"About time!" he said as Shane drove up and parked next to the creek. He'd called in a favor when he realized the repair job had gotten away from him, and Shane had agreed to pop over to help. "I expected you an hour ago."

"Sorry," Shane said. "Thought we could use some more reinforcements."

The truck doors opened, and Noah and Ryder climbed out.

"What're you doing here?" Josh asked as they retrieved their tools from the bed of the truck.

"Heard you'd decided to remodel the property instead of dealing with your feelings," Noah said, walking over and clapping him on the shoulder.

Josh glared at Shane. "Really?"

"Look, I didn't tell them everything. The details are for you to disclose," Shane reasoned. "I just needed some backup."

"Because clearly you and Amy are having troubles," Ryder said, "and it's bumming you out, man."

"It's not bumming me out," Josh muttered.

"You're bummed." Ryder took him by the cheeks and looked back at the others. "Isn't this the face of a man who's bummed?"

"Never seen anyone more bummed," Noah agreed.

Josh shrugged him off. He wasn't bummed. He was devastated, but he didn't really want to get into that. The whole point of this job was to get his mind off Amy, not talk about her even more. "I can't believe you brought these two fools with you," he muttered to Shane.

"I can't play relationship expert all by myself," Shane told him as he grabbed a board from Josh's truck and carried it over. "I needed someone with more experience getting rejected." He dropped the board in place and nudged Ryder. "Right?"

Ryder scoffed. "Not funny, man."

Shane steered Ryder in Josh's direction. "Here is your walking, talking example of what not to do in these kinds of situations."

"I'll have you know, I'm happily single," Ryder said. He gestured to Josh. "Does this man look happy to you? He's way past my tried-and-true method of 'get in and get out before the feelings get their hooks in you.'"

"Agreed," Noah said, hammering nails into the board Shane had just placed. "He's been hooked."

Ryder set off for another board, and Shane leveled Josh with a stare. "I know this isn't what you were expecting today," he said, readjusting his Stetson. "But this way we get the bridge repaired faster, and maybe you'll listen to someone else since clearly you didn't take my brilliant advice."

"What brilliant advice?" Josh said. "You gave me two options the other night. You said I could walk away or I could fight for her."

Shane gave him a *duh!* look. "And what exactly are you doing?"

"Well, I'm… I'm…" Josh put his hands on his hips, staring off at the cattle in the distance. What the hell *was* he doing?

"That's what I mean," Shane said. "You clearly haven't walked away from Amy. And you're not over her. So why aren't you out there trying to make this work?"

"Because I don't know how to make this work," Josh said with a grunt. He wasn't a star-studded, high-rolling movie star, and he didn't know how to prove to Amy that he could offer her more than Tru ever could. Tru would always be wealthier. He'd always be famous. He'd always be this baby's biological father. And just because Amy had said that Tru walked away didn't mean things were over between them. Tru could have a change of heart, decide he wanted to know his child, and maybe Amy would fall for that charming smile all over again.

"Look, it's a little difficult to give you advice when I don't know what's going on," Noah said.

Josh sighed. These were his best friends. And the news was bound to come out sometime. He trusted them enough to hold their tongues until it did. "She's pregnant."

Ryder barked a laugh, giving Josh's shoulders a squeeze. "You two made quick work of that."

"It's not mine."

"Damn," Ryder said, his tone shifting from congratulatory to conflicted. "Sorry. I didn't even think."

"You don't often before you open your mouth," Noah said to him.

"No, it's okay," Josh cut in before Ryder could respond. "It was a shock to all parties involved."

"So, that's what this is all about, then?" Noah continued. "Why things are so complicated?"

"Exactly. I was serious about Amy. I *am* serious about her. But now there's this baby and her ex, and I just don't know where I fit into that picture."

"So, the other guy's still around?" Ryder said.

Josh hummed. "I mean… He was. But I'm not so sure anymore."

"Has he asked you to back off?" Noah asked.

"No."

"Has Amy asked you to back off?" Shane clarified.

"No," Josh said again.

Ryder ran his hand through his hair, scratching at the back of his head. "Okay, I know I'm not exactly the person to be asking about committed relationships here, but seems to me like you want Amy, she wants you, and instead of making that happen, you're sitting here with your cattle. Have I got that right?"

"That's not what's happening," Josh said.

"That's exactly what's happening," Shane muttered.

"Sounds to me like you're feeling sorry for yourself," Noah said. "You need to knock that off, follow your heart and go get your girl back."

Josh huffed. Last time he'd followed his heart, Erica had stomped on it on her way out of town.

"You got company coming?" Shane asked as a car turned onto the property.

Josh whipped his phone out of his pocket and checked the time. Had the day really gotten away from him that quickly? He'd been expecting visitors, he'd just planned to be a little less sweaty when they arrived. "Yeah, actually. I've got a meeting."

"Then I guess we'll let you off the hook for now," Ryder said, poking Josh playfully in the chest. "But next time we talk, you better have good news for us."

"You just focus on yourself," Josh said. "I heard you're cycling through women so fast your mother's stopped asking their names."

Noah snickered, leading Ryder back to Shane's truck.

"Call me later," Shane said. "I'll come out and help you finish up."

"Thanks," Josh said. "And thanks for this, I guess." He wasn't really in the mood for advice, but Shane's heart was in the right place.

"Just sit with what we said for a while," Shane said. "You'll figure it out."

"If you say so." Josh waved as they left, then quickly packed up his tools and the excess lumber. He tossed it all into the bed of his pickup and drove over to the house. Mike

Cooper had messaged him earlier in the day, asking if it was okay for Stanley Sanchez to swing by. He wanted to follow up about the conversation Mike and Josh had at the Tenacity Social Club regarding the rocks on the old Woodson property. Josh didn't know how he'd found himself in the middle of Stanley's investigation, and he wasn't sure what kind of help he could be in the search for the Deroy family, but he'd agreed to talk to the man. He figured it was another way to keep his mind off Amy, though clearly his friends were determined to keep his thoughts there anyway.

He sighed, getting out of his truck.

"Hey there!" a man called, stepping out of his vehicle. He was older than Josh had expected, tufts of white hair visible under his black cowboy hat. He wore denim on denim and a leather vest.

"Hi," Josh said. He headed over to greet him.

The man stuck out his hand. "Stanley Sanchez."

Josh shook his hand. "Josh Aventura. Good to meet you. Mike said you'd be coming by."

A door thudded and Josh looked up to see a woman come around the vehicle.

"This is my grandniece, Nina," Stanley said.

Josh recognized her as the daughter of Tenacity locals Will and Nicole Sanchez. She was tall, with dark hair that reminded him of Amy. And a smile that reminded him of Amy. And...this not thinking about Amy thing was not going so well.

"Hi," she said, smiling at him. "Hope we're not interrupting your work."

"No." Josh glanced over his shoulder. "I mean, there's always work but that doesn't mean I couldn't do with a break. So, Mike said you wanted to talk about what I told him?"

"Firstly we wanted to thank you for giving Mike that tip

and for your part in helping us find 'Juniper Rock,'" Stanley said.

"You found what you were looking for then?" Josh said.

Stanley tipped his head back and forth. "The people who live there now are not keen to let us on the property. I think they got spooked by the word *investigation*."

"Right," Josh said. The Stoolers weren't the chattiest of neighbors as far as Josh was concerned, but they'd always seemed reasonable. Then again, if someone told Josh they were investigating and wanted to poke around his property, he might have gotten weirded out too. "That's too bad."

"We were hoping that you might be able to pave the way for us," Nina said. "You being neighbors and all."

"What we find there could end up having ramifications for the whole town," Stanley added.

Ramifications for the whole town? That seemed like a good enough reason to try. Besides, what did Josh have to lose? He had no stake in the game. And if he helped a neighbor in the end… "I don't know them well," Josh cautioned. "They're quiet neighbors. Mostly keep to themselves. So I'm not promising any miracles, but I'll give it my best shot."

Nina grinned so wide it made him think of Amy again and his chest ached. "Great!" She clapped her hands together. "You have no idea how much this means."

Josh glanced down at his sweaty, dusty clothes. "I'm gonna change real quick. Probably better to make a good impression if they've already turned you down once. I'll be right back. Then we have to make a pit stop."

"We did all that for some mac and cheese? I don't see how this is going to help," Nina said as they arrived on the Stooler property. It hadn't changed much since it belonged to the Woodsons from what Josh could remember. There was a large barn at the back of the property and a pair of tall silos and a long, winding drive that disappeared to a massive garage. Josh held a tray of Angela's mac and cheese in his hands.

"This isn't just any mac and cheese. This is the best in all of Montana," Josh said. "Trust me. If that doesn't convince the Stoolers to let you have a little look around the property, then nothing will. Plus I practically had to sell Angela my soul to get this." And dodge a lot of awkward questions about where Amy was. Shane had been tight-lipped about Josh's woes and that had just made Angela more suspicious. She'd given him the *look*—the same look his mother would have given him if she was in town—and Josh had felt the combined weight of Angela's disappointment mingle with his own.

"Well," Nina said, "let's hope this magic dish does the trick."

They walked up to the door, with Josh flanked by the Sanchezes, and he felt like a kid again, dragged into one of Shane's silly schemes. Nina rang the doorbell, and they waited. Josh didn't know why *he* was so nervous. A moment later, the door opened.

Mr. Stooler looked back at him, lifting the reading glasses off the end of his nose. He looked past Josh to glare at Stanley and Nina. "I thought I already told you two I wasn't interested in having people poke around my property."

"We don't mean to give you any trouble," Nina said. "Honest. I'm just trying to figure out what happened to someone I really cared a lot about."

Mr. Stooler didn't look convinced by her plea.

"Fifteen minutes," Josh said. "That's all we're asking. Then we'll be out of your hair. And as a thank-you, I've got some of Angela Corey's mac and cheese here." Josh lifted the tray, making his offering.

Mr. Stooler's eyes darted to the tray. "Angela's, huh?"

Josh bit down on his grin. This dish really was magical.

"Darrel, just let them look around already!" a woman called from inside the house. "What do you care about the rocks at the edge of the property anyway?"

Mrs. Stooler came to the door, two heads shorter than her husband, but with the attitude to make up for it. She took the tray of mac and cheese from Josh. "Thank you. This was a lovely gesture. You didn't have to do this." She nodded toward the driveway. "Well, go on and have a look. Take as long as you need."

Mr. Stooler gave them all a gruff nod. "I'll come out and join y'all in a minute."

Stanley tipped his hat. "We're mighty grateful. Won't be long."

They turned and the door closed behind them. "Let's make it quick," Josh whispered to Stanley. "In case Mr. Stooler changes his mind."

They marched off down the driveway, to the very edge of the property line, where large rocks were piled up, some as tall as him. Josh remembered driving past as a kid, watching the Woodson boy climb on them.

Stanley and Nina separated, inspecting the different groupings. Josh stared after them as they started to feel around in the grooves.

"What exactly are we looking for?" he asked.

"We'll know it when we see it," Stanley said.

Josh laughed and shook his head. "Sure." He wandered between the rocks, his mind drifting to Amy. He wondered what she was up to today. How she was feeling. If things with Tru were still status quo. He missed her. He wanted to hear her voice more than anything.

He reached for his phone almost without thinking.

Stanley picked up a long stick and started tapping on some of the smaller rocks, bending close to listen to the sounds.

What would he even say if he called? *How are you* seemed rather empty when what he really wanted to say was *I miss you and I want you.*

Stanley tapped along another batch of rocks and froze when one echoed back strangely.

Josh slipped his phone back into his pocket and joined him. Nina hurried over. The rock was about as high as Josh's knee. "False bottom?" he said.

"Sounds like it." Stanley gripped one side of the rock. "Give me a hand here."

Together, Josh and Nina helped Stanley shove the rock over, exposing what was very clearly a false addition to the stone based on the color difference. Stanley whipped out a small pocketknife that dangled from his key ring and pried the bottom open.

The metal creaked and groaned, rusty after all that time of sitting in the wet earth.

When the bottom flew off, Nina gasped. Inside was a wadded-up roll of money and a folded-up note. She reached in and carefully unfolded the paper. She cleared her throat, reading it out loud. "'You got the wrong man.'"

"Well, I'll be damned," Stanley said.

"Do you think this means Barrett didn't do it?" Nina said. She sounded on the verge of tears.

"I think the only thing we can be sure of is that someone believed they'd accused the wrong man," Stanley said. "And that's enough to question everything."

"What d'you got there?" Mr. Stooler called, walking over. He spied the roll of money in Stan's hand. "My God." His eyes widened. "That should be ours, now. You hear? It was found on our property."

"We'll have to turn the funds over to the authorities," Stanley said. "It's evidence. Once that's cleared, they can decide who to allocate it to."

Mr. Stooler huffed a bit, but he couldn't argue that logic.

Stanley rose to his feet. "You want me to call them out to take a look or will you?"

"Suppose I'll do it," Mr. Stooler said. "It's my land anyhow." He inclined his head and he and Stanley set off for the house.

Josh smiled as Nina smothered a grin behind her hand. She was still defending Barrett after all these years. "You do know that it's still possible that Barrett could have put the money—and that note—there himself."

Nina solemnly shook her head. "I've always thought that the Deroys' sudden departure from Tenacity made no sense. And I'm choosing to believe that this note proves Barrett never would have done something so horrible to the town. I know there's still so much more to the investigation but—"

"All these years later, you still have that much faith in him?" Josh asked.

She tilted her head, a funny little smile coming over her face. "Yes. Do you still have faith in you and Amy?"

Josh flinched. He knew Tenacity was a small town, he just didn't realize how fast word about him and Amy had spread. He supposed they'd been seen out together…a lot. And he'd been hanging around the feed store more than necessary. Still, he was a little surprised that Nina knew about their relationship.

"I obviously don't know exactly what's going on with you two, but you really do look miserable."

Josh sighed. "Can't deny that."

"Why don't you go do something about it?"

Josh laughed despite himself. "It's that easy, huh?"

"It *is* that easy. Well," she smirked, "it's a hell of a lot easier than unearthing false-bottomed boulders on the Stoolers' property."

She was right about that. And about Amy. Heck, it was the same thing Shane, Ryder and Noah had tried to tell him earlier, he'd just been too stubborn and miserable to listen. But maybe he'd just needed these little nudges in the right direction to get his act together. Because if the guys were telling him to go for it and Nina was still fighting for Barrett after all this time, then he could sure as hell fight for Amy.

He excused himself from Nina, took out his phone and dialed. But it wasn't Amy he called. Not at first. It was his mother.

"About time, Joshua!" she said when she answered the phone. "Your father's just about eaten his weight in pickled herring and every time we stop in a port, I get an update from Iris Strom. First you and Amy are seeing each other. Then you're not."

"I'm hopefully about to change that," Josh said.

"What's going on?"

"I've been a fool and it's taken me this long to screw my head on straight, but I felt like I needed to talk to you and Dad first, so you don't think I'm jumping into something without thinking it through first."

"That's not like you," his mother said. "Why would we think that?"

"Because… I want to be with Amy. I want to make a life with her." The truth was, he wanted Amy, even if she'd chosen someone else first, even if he'd only ever be her second choice. He might not be able to hold a candle to Tru McCoy, but he wanted to take care of her and her child. He thought that she could be happy with him, and that they could have a good life together. And maybe those were all foolish things to think, and she'd reject him anyway, but he knew what his heart wanted, and he at least needed to try.

"Oh, Josh! That's music to my ears."

"But there's something you should know." Josh swallowed. There wasn't really a delicate way to break this news. "Amy's pregnant."

His mother gasped.

"It's not mine," he rushed to say before she could get carried away. "But I... I want it to be. I know we've only just met, and I haven't even introduced her to you and Dad yet, but she's the one. I *know* she is. And I want to raise this baby as my own. If Amy will have me, that is."

He stopped talking, taking in the silence on the other end of the line.

"Do you think I'm still being a fool?" he asked.

"Do you love this girl?" his mother replied.

"Yes," Josh said. "More than anything."

"Then that's all that matters."

"But do you think I'm ready to be a dad?"

His mother chuckled softly. "Josh, none of us is ever ready. Look at me and your father. You showed up later in life and we still weren't ready. But we loved you, and we figured it out. And you and Amy will, too. Remember what your father told you? All that really matters at the end of the day is that you have good people to call home. That's all we've ever wanted for you. So, if you've found your person, you hold on to her tight. Right?"

"Right," he said, fighting the emotion that swirled in his chest.

"Now, you go fix things with Amy," his mother said. "Because I want to meet my grandbaby when the time comes."

Josh laughed, pressing his hand to his forehead. Maybe he'd only been looking for Ms. Right Now before meeting

Amy, but she was Mrs. Right…his Mrs. Forever. He knew it down to his boots. She was the only one for him. And the old Josh might have let her go without a word and retreated back into his world of cattle, but it was time to risk his heart again and go after what would make him truly happy.

"Oh, I can't wait to tell your father! He's going to be thrilled. We both are, Josh. We love you."

"Love you, too, Mom."

"Call me later with good news?"

"You bet." Josh hung up, finally ready to call Amy, adrenaline surging through him. He sure hoped he'd be calling his mother back with good news. His hands shook as he found Amy's number in his call log. He hit Dial.

Part of him worried she might not take his call, but she answered after the second ring.

"Hi," he said.

"Hey there, cowboy," she answered, a mix of surprise and relief in her voice.

"Do you think we can meet up in person?" he asked. "To talk?"

There was a pause. "Where?"

"The ranch?" Josh suggested. At least there they'd have privacy.

"Okay," Amy agreed. "I'll see you soon."

Chapter Twenty

Amy felt like a shaken soda bottle as she turned off Juniper Road and down the gravel drive leading to Split Valley Ranch. Nerves coiled in her gut, and her hands trembled against the steering wheel of her car. The shakes were so bad by the time she pulled up beside the house that she had to sit in the driver's seat and take a few deep, calming breaths. In through her nose. Out through her mouth. And again. In and out.

Elizabeth had told her to fight for him, and she'd wanted to call him for days. But that fear of rejection had planted itself inside her chest and refused to move. Every time she'd tried to pick up the phone, she'd been overwhelmed with the image of Josh pulling away, of him turning his back on her. So she'd resigned herself to giving him more time. She tried not to take up space in his world even though that's all she wanted to do. That didn't stop her from missing him though.

She'd done her best to keep busy with Faith and the feed store and planning for this baby. There was so much to do. So many unknowns. She was grateful for all her sisters and the constant stream of parenting and relationship advice trickling down the group chat since their lunch at Lulu's. She'd missed them and had loved seeing them, but truthfully, she'd found herself missing Tenacity even more. She'd missed the small-town happenings and the quiet and seeing the same people day in and day out. She used to love the city. When had her heart shifted?

The moment I met Josh, she told herself.

She missed him everywhere. Sitting on the porch in the evenings with tea and toast. Bumping into customers in aisles in the store. Mostly she missed being here with him, riding through the pastures, nothing for miles but them and the Montana skyline.

She touched her belly.

There would be no more riding for a while.

And there might not be any more Josh after today.

That last thought churned in her stomach worse than any morning sickness. If Josh had come to the conclusion that he simply couldn't raise another man's baby, this would be the end of them.

Amy blinked, fighting off tears. *Dammit*. If she started crying now, she'd never be able to stop. She'd be a blubbering mess before Josh even uttered a hello. *If* he said hello. She'd been playing out this moment in her mind, trying to anticipate what Josh might have to say. Amy fought the urge to believe that he'd leave her like Tru, but unlike with Tru, she'd understand. Josh hadn't signed up to be a father to someone else's kid. And regardless of what they wanted, Amy was about to be a mother. Tears grew heavy in the corners of her eyes. She swiped at them with her fingers. *Get it together, Amy.*

This news had blown in like a twister, disrupting both their lives, and it wasn't fair of her to expect Josh to pick up those pieces or to try to salvage this relationship. She imagined the situation in reverse. What if Josh had sprung a kid on her? To fall for someone only to watch their past creep back in and change everything you thought you knew about them. Her first instinct might have been to step away too.

She supposed there was no more putting it off though. It was time to find out if there was anything left to fight for. Amy climbed out of the car and walked around the side of the house, up the porch steps.

Josh leaned against the railing, looking out at the barn. He had a beer in his hand. He left the bottle on the railing the moment he spotted her. "You came!"

"Of course I came." She noticed a few more beers scattered about. *Uh-oh.* Had Josh needed some liquid courage before dropping the news that this was over? Her heart gave a dull, hollow thump, and she resisted the urge to rub at the spot where her chest ached. Fear made it difficult to swallow, and heaviness welled behind her eyes. She didn't know if she wanted to scream or cry or curse Tru McCoy until the cows came home.

"How are you?" he asked.

"Good." Her gaze drifted past him briefly. "Having a bit of a party?"

He looked over his shoulder at the empty beer bottles. "Oh, no. More like a celebration, I guess. I, uh, got roped into some detective work with Stanley Sanchez and his grandniece, Nina. We were just celebrating a clue that panned out. Sort of a big deal for the town. At least, Stan says so."

Amy's eyes widened. Of all the things she imagined Josh doing in their time apart, detective work was not one of them.

Josh shook his head. "Anyway, I'll tell you about it later."

Amy's heart startled to life, rattling with anticipation. More than anything she wanted them to *have* a later.

"That's not what I called you over to talk about," Josh continued.

Right. Was this it? Should she prepare herself for the

blow? Amy wasn't sure anything could prepare her. She'd been hurt by Tru, but losing Josh would be different. It would devastate her. She hadn't wanted to admit that to herself, hadn't wanted to face the heartbreak before she had to, but now there was nowhere to hide.

"How is the…" Josh looked down between them, his voice softening. "How is the baby?"

"Baby's doing well." She flattened her hand against her stomach. "I had an appointment with a doctor the other day." Did he even want to know these things if this was over? His eyes found hers and held them. "Up in Bronco. She did a bunch of tests. Everything's right on track."

"That's great news. Did you get… I mean… Is it too soon for an ultrasound?"

"Doc gave me one." She cleared her throat. "I got to hear the heartbeat." *I wanted you to hear it too. I wished you were there, seeing this baby. Our baby?*

Josh's hands tightened around her elbows. "And the doc said it sounded good?"

"She said everything's perfect. I worried a bit, not having realized I was pregnant, that I might have hurt the baby hauling around stuff at the feed store or riding around on Bitsy. But she said everything's okay. Just no more horseback riding until this little one comes."

"Guess we'll have to find something else to keep you occupied on the ranch."

Amy opened her mouth, closed it. Did he mean that or was he trying to let her down easy?

"I'm sorry it took me so long to call," Josh said. "Truly."

"No, it's okay… It's…" Her voice broke, and Josh reached for her, gathering her into his arms. Amy melted against him. The embrace felt right, like coming home, and her insides twisted so painfully she just barely managed to bite back a sob. She was clinging to a thread of hope, but this reunion still felt so tentative. Would Josh really hold her like this while ending things?

"I wanted to call you every day. But every time I picked up my phone, I chickened out." He wove his fingers through hers. "Who knew something so simple could be so scary?"

"I assumed all this time that you had been questioning whether you could raise another man's child. Or whether you even wanted to have kids at all. That's a big question to answer. So I wanted to give you time and space to think about it, or else I would have called too."

"I've known for a while now that I wanted a family. A wife. A couple kids running around the ranch, hearing their laughter spill across the pasture. Keeping them from getting up to mischief." He chuckled softly to himself. "Well, some of it, at least."

Amy let out a strangled breath, swiping at the single tear that slipped free. He painted a beautiful picture, but just because he wanted a wife and kids didn't mean he wanted her. "If it wasn't the baby that kept you away, then was it me?"

"God, no, Amy!" He cupped her jaw, running his thumb over her cheek. "Mostly I was thinking that it's a little hard to compete when your opponent is an internationally renowned heartthrob. I can't jet you off to private islands or shower you with luxuries. Not the way Tru could. And I guess I didn't feel good enough for you. I also sort of thought that by fighting for you, I might be depriving you of the life you and this baby could have had with Tru."

"Good enough for me?" Amy practically choked on the words. "Oh, Josh. You're *too* good for me if anything."

"Amy—"

"I'm serious." Amy couldn't believe that's what he'd been worrying about. "Tru and the jet-setting were a distraction from what I really wanted out of life. It was never real. It was never going to be anything. We were never going to work."

"So what do you really want out of life?"

"Someone solid and down-to-earth. Someone who's going to be there for me, that *wants* to be there for me." Not someone that was running around the globe, chasing fame. At one point she'd thought that Tru was something special, but now she knew he wasn't a real hero. He wasn't the kind of guy who would tend to her when she was sick, or make her laugh till she cried, or even ask her what she was thinking. "Until I met you, I didn't even realize what I was missing out on. And now, I can't imagine my life without you. I know that's a selfish thing to say, considering the circumstances."

"It's not," Josh assured her. "I promise it's not."

Amy plowed on. Whatever happened now, at least she could say she'd told Josh exactly how she felt. "I've done a lot of thinking lately, and the globe-trotting life is fine, for some. Maybe even for me, once upon a time. But that was then, and this is now. Now I want a quiet life…with you. Something simple and happy."

"Amy, that's all I wa—"

"Wait," she said. "Please. I just want to say that I also understand if you don't want to be a parent to this baby. I know you said you want kids, but maybe you want your own children, and that's okay. But I *am* going to have this baby, and if you're not all in, I won't hold it against you. It's a big change and a lot of responsibility in a short amount of time. It's asking for twice the commitment and we both know how new this still is between us. There is no pressure." Everything shook—her voice as she forced the words out, her hands where they clutched his sides, her chest as her heart rattled uncontrollably. She was almost dizzied by the intensity of her feelings. By how much these words hurt her to say. "We can part as friends."

"No," Josh said immediately. "We can't be friends."

Amy just looked at him, silently wishing and pleading, wanting him to choose her.

"I'm not young and naïve," he continued. "I spent a long time looking after a piece of land, wondering what my dad really meant when he said all that mattered is having good people to call home. But now I finally understand. You're my home, Amy. I know it's soon, but I also know my mind and my heart, and I love you too much to ever let us just be friends. And I will love this baby too, if you'll let me. So, in case it's not clear yet, I'm all in."

"Josh—" Her voice trembled.

"And I've already told my mom you're my person. She's really excited to meet you." He grinned. "Please don't make me go back on my word."

A laugh of disbelief tore up her throat, and Amy dove into his arms. This time she couldn't stop the tears that flooded down her cheeks. They were happy tears, though. Tears of joy. She tilted her face up and kissed him. Again and again. She kissed him in a way that hopefully told him there was no one else in the world for her.

She kissed him until he knew just how much she loved him too.

Chapter Twenty-One

Josh kissed her back, feeling her lips part in a gasp. It felt like it had been ages since he'd kissed her, and he sank into her touch like a starving man into a meal. He wanted to devour her. To make her tremble in his arms. To make up for all the moments he'd made her question his intentions.

Josh deepened the kiss until it was all tongue and teeth, soft and sweet. When Amy finally turned her head to gasp for air, he pulled back, giving them both some space.

"Is this okay?" he asked, stroking his thumbs along her cheekbones. There were unshed tears in her eyes. "Are you... Are you okay?"

She nodded, her smile watery. "It's better than okay."

"You're sure?"

She laughed a little. "I'm just so happy."

"Good," he said, pecking her on the lips again. "I want to keep making you happy, for as long as you'll let me."

"I mean it, Josh," she said, her hand pressing gently against his chest, her fingertips brushing over the place where his heart beat. "*You* make me so happy."

Josh wanted to laugh and scream and cry. He didn't know where to start first. Mostly he just planned to keep kissing her. Then he was going to make Amy feel all the ways in which he wanted her. He was going to make her feel good and safe. He was going to make sure she knew that she belonged with him and only him.

Her and her baby.

"Come inside?" he asked, his voice low.

She bit her bottom lip, grinning as he kissed her cheek, nuzzling against her. "Why? You have something fun in mind, cowboy?"

"I think I could come up with an activity that we might both enjoy."

"Oh, yeah?" She slid her hand beneath his shirt, her fingers sliding around to his back, smoothing across his skin. "Dinner and a movie?"

"Not quite."

"Too bad. I'm quite ravenous."

"Well, I'm ravenous for something else."

Amy giggled as he pulled her close, kissing his way down her neck.

He hummed against her, feeling more than hearing the soft sigh that left her lips.

She smiled at him. No, she beamed at him, and Josh knew right then that he wanted to spend the rest of his life waking up beside that smile. Amy followed him through the door. He closed it after her, and she surprised him by pressing him up against the back of the door. She ran her hands up his chest and over his shoulders, lifting up on her toes to whisper her lips along his jaw.

"God, I missed you," he grumbled.

"I missed you more."

"Not possible." Sure he'd missed this, but it was more than that. He'd missed having Amy in his space. He wanted traces of her in the bathroom and touches of her in the living room. He wanted to find her books left by the couch and her dishes in the sink and her hair ties around the gearshift in his truck.

And one day soon he wanted to be tripping over baby toys and looking for the last clean bottle in the middle of the night. He wanted to live that life with her. That hectic, crazy life filled with so much love that he'd gladly lie awake all night just listening to these people breathe.

He wanted little feet on the stairs and in the barn. He wanted this family so much it was a pain between his ribs.

"You okay?" Amy asked, looking up at him.

"I'm perfect," he said. He caught her hand and kissed every one of her fingers. Then he nudged her with his hips, and Amy backed them toward the couch, stripping out of her clothes.

"Thought we were aiming for the bedroom?"

"You should have known we were never going to make it that far," Amy laughed. She tugged Josh down to the couch and climbed into his lap.

Josh took his time with her, lingering in places that made her squirm and listening to the way her breath hitched as his fingers danced across her skin. He was gentle and reverential and unhurried, knowing, somehow, that they had forever to do this now. He had all the time in the world to worship her the way he wanted, to love her.

Amy threw her head back, and he lavished her neck with kisses.

"Touch me," she begged. "*Please.*"

So he did. When they came together Amy let out a pretty little sigh and Josh echoed it, relieved as the blood rushed past his ears.

He moved against her and Amy moved against him, finding a rhythm that worked, that left them both wanting more, and when Amy cried out, Josh stilled long enough to watch her unravel. It was quickly becoming one of his favorite sights in the world.

Josh followed her into oblivion a moment later, then pulled her close, simply breathing in the moment as bliss washed through him.

They lay like that for a while, Amy tracing patterns into his forearm, humming contentedly whenever he pressed a kiss to her shoulder. She shivered as he ran his stubbled chin over her soft skin.

"That feels nice," she murmured.

He reached up and kissed the space behind her ear, then her throat, then shifted, so she was lying beneath him.

He studied her face.

All he saw there was contentment. How had he gotten so lucky?

Amy ran her hands through his hair, smoothing it back from his forehead. "What are you thinking?"

"That one day I'll be old and you'll be gray, and I'll still be looking at you like this."

Amy opened her mouth but no words came out. Instead she kissed him again, softly, stirring warmth in his gut. "That sounds lovely."

Josh wormed his way down her body, pressing his hand to her belly. Her breath hitched again as he kissed her stomach. There was a small, soft bump and he considered the fact that he was going to be a father to this baby. He grinned against Amy's stomach. He thought about how Amy had healed the wounded part of his heart, the same way he'd proven that she could trust him, and how wonderful it was that he'd found someone content to share this simple little life with him.

"I can still feel you thinking very hard," she said.

"I want us to be married before the baby comes." He heard her sharp intake of breath. "So the child can have my name."

Her lips twisted. "Is that a proposal, Josh Aventura?"

"It will be, if it's something you want?"

Amy hummed happily. "I think I could warm up to the idea."

"Only warm up to it?" he said, climbing back up her body. She giggled as he took her in his arms, nibbling at her neck. "You know, I didn't think I'd be able to give you a life filled with adventure, but now I think that life with you and our baby"—their baby!— "will be the best damn adventure either of us has ever gone on."

Amy looked at him, her eyes glassy. She pressed her hand to his cheek. "I would marry you tomorrow, but maybe we should wait until we can arrange for the families to be here."

"How about next month?"

Amy laughed. "Eager there, cowboy?"

"Eager to spend all the days of my life calling you my wife."

Amy kissed him again. "What am I going to do with you?"

"Hopefully many wonderful things," he said, eyeing her in a way that made them both laugh. And he smiled, knowing he would get to hear that laughter every day for the rest of his life.

Twilight spilled across Tenacity, painting the Strom and Son Feed and Farm Supply sign in soft yellow shadows. The bell rang over the door in the feed store as Josh pushed inside, Amy right behind him. He'd hardly let her go since she showed up at the ranch, her hand still entwined with his own.

"You sure you want to do this now?"

"Yes." She squeezed his hand and he could feel her certainty and her joy radiate through him. Josh didn't think he'd stopped floating all afternoon. He was going to be a husband and a father.

"We're closing up shortly!" he heard Caleb call from somewhere in the store.

"So make it snappy," Faith added.

"It's just us," Amy called.

"Us?" Faith poked her head out of an aisle, a massive grin splitting her face as she eyeballed their joined hands. "Us as in…"

"We talked," Amy said. "Sorted ourselves out."

"Thank God." Faith came toward them. "Caleb, get out here! It's about damn time."

Josh chuckled at her antics. "Made some big decisions, too."

"Oh?" Faith said as Caleb jogged over.

"What's happening?" he asked, breathless.

"Big things supposedly," Faith said.

"In that case," Caleb waved them over to the cash desk, "step into our office. And tell us all about these big decisions."

Amy sucked in a breath, then let it out as she announced, "We're getting married."

Faith put her hand to her forehead and feigned shock.

Amy broke down laughing and hugged her sister. "You out of anyone should not be surprised. You've been meddling in this relationship the entire time."

"She is very good at meddling," Caleb said, pecking Faith on the temple with his lips.

"Because I could see this moment coming from a mile away," Faith agreed. She squeezed Amy tightly. "Congratulations. I'm so happy for you." She reached for Josh, finding his hand. "And for you too."

Amy pulled away as Caleb clapped Josh on the shoulder. "We need to tell the families, obviously. And it'll probably be a small, quick little thing." She glanced at Josh and he nodded. That suited him just fine. If Amy wanted a fuss, he'd give her a fuss, but he was just as happy with something small. Something with their favorite people and each other. "But you'll be my maid of honor?" Amy continued.

"Of course," Faith said. "The others would have had to fight me for it."

Amy chuckled.

"Sure you're gonna be able to handle *all* the Hawkins sisters?" Caleb asked Josh. "They can be a lot."

He reached for Amy and pulled her close. "I think it'll be one hell of an adventure."

* * * * *

Don't miss the next installment of the new continuity
Montana Mavericks: The Tenacity Social Club

A Maverick Worth Waiting For
by USA TODAY *bestselling author Laurel Greer*
On sale May 2025, wherever Harlequin books
and ebooks are sold.

And look for the previous book in the series,

A Maverick's Road Home
by USA TODAY *bestselling author Catherine Mann*

Available now!